Catching the Horizon

by Josh Carroll

978-0-578-00636-9

Catching the Horizon is dedicated to everybody who supported my vision along the way. In particular, to the countless people who volunteered to read sections, to proofread, and to offer insight. Thank you for your patience and understanding.

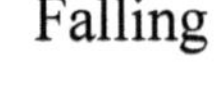

Falling

12/25/01

My mother's already staring at the Christmas tree from the couch with her blue robe dangling around her scant waist and her fluffy, blue slippers perched precariously on the glass coffee table. She is waiting for us to emerge to open the splendor that is Christmas from beneath the tree. My brothers and I awake nearly simultaneously and hover over our piles like vultures eyeing a feast.

As I open presents from Santa, Frosty, and Rudolph—watching my mom muse over her creativity—most of this stuff I don't want or need, what 15-year-old boy really wants a toy rocking horse? But I can't ask for what I really want and still live. Yet I pretend to love everything and that makes Mom smile. And that's all that counts, my mom's smiling. She's never really done a lot of that.

My older brother keeps tossing his presents aside and my younger brother questions, "Is that it?" The smile starts to fade from Mom's eyes and I want to knock both of them out. But they save themselves by laughing it off and handing Mom their presents. Her smile's returned and everything is all right again.

Listening to the songs at mass gives me time to think about all of the happy families strolling into the pews. Ours is different—there's no father to smile proudly at the end of the row. I feel like everyone's always looking at me during mass wondering if we're bastards or not, especially God; does He judge us? I want to run out of this place, but that'll just justify their beliefs. These thoughts race through my mind, I lose my breath and now my skin's burning and my nerves are twitching and I find myself gasping for breath while my stomach turns over in my throat. I've felt this way before, but usually not in public. I don't want to be different, and I fear everybody around me sees me as different. Surviving the hour of solemnity wears me out and I just want to lie on the couch all day while Mom makes Christmas dinner for us and a few family friends. And we all pretend to be happy.

12/26/01

We have to go to my dad's house today to celebrate Christmas with him, my step-mom, and half brother. My older brother Mark drives us up there. He's a freshman in college and thinks that he's come home to be my boss. Mark hates our step-mom and disapproves of our father. I have to listen to him complain about how much our family sucks and how Lois ruined our lives and our dad's worthless. Layne sleeps in the back seat and avoids this tirade. But I don't. He asks me what I think about all of this.

I want to tell him that I love my dad and I don't hate Lois. I know my parents getting divorced wasn't all her fault. I want to tell Mark that Dad loves him and takes care of him. After all, he always says he loves us and never misses anything important, plus he's paying for college. But I don't tell him this. I tried telling him that over Thanksgiving, but he told me I was talking stupid and I was an idiot and all of that other stuff didn't matter. He told me Dad ruined his life and childhood—but I don't see that.

So I say nothing, and Mark just continues to lash out about our dad ruining his life and how he wishes Lois never existed.

Sometimes, I wish Mark never existed.

I can't help but feel all of the hugs we exchange with one another as we walk through the door are phony. Lois hugs all of us and so does Dad. Layne seems pleased and I don't really care either way. But Mark seems all tense and I can't believe he's hugging the very people he hated so much just a few minutes ago.

Devon's Christmas pile seems ten times bigger than mine. But he's my step-mom's only son so I guess she spoils him. Plus Dad says it's really the same amount of stuff we get from him and our Mom combined, it's just under one tree so it looks bigger. Yet Devon has a guitar, amp, and stereo stashed under the tree while I open an ugly green sweater. I know I shouldn't be jealous and other kids have far less than me. But I am. And the sad part is I know Devon feels guilty too. He doesn't even really want to tell us what he got for Christmas. So we avoid the topic and eat another Christmas dinner trying to pretend it's the first Christmas dinner. But we all know it's not.

As we eat, my dad seems to be in his glory. He steals the conversation repeating the same stories we've heard for years. His red faced-laugh at his own stories always ends with a tear dripping from under his glasses as he chokes out 'how great it is to have everyone together.' Lois nods in agreement and we all fall into line by agreeing out loud. It's Mark's insides that disagree and I'm feeling nervous again because I'm afraid he might say his true feelings out loud and Christmas would be ruined. But he doesn't. And we all pretend to be happy.

12/27/01

On the way back to Mom's house, Mark's tirade begins anew, this time ending with how he's not even going up there next year. Nothing went wrong, I think, but to him the whole trip was a disaster. I haven't figured out why yet. I wish I could sleep like Layne; sometimes I wonder if he's just pretending so he doesn't have to get involved.

12/31/01

Every year we try a new restaurant for New Year's Eve dinner. Usually Mom picks the restaurant and we dine like we're rich for one night. After dinner my brothers and I will go our separate ways to separate festivities, but Mom will go home and watch the ball drop on television. I wish she would go out and do something. Every year several of her friends ask her here or there, but she always declines. I wonder why. She says she would rather watch from the peace and quiet of her home. But she watches every night. I wish she would at least try going out.

For dinner tonight, Mom's chosen a relatively new restaurant right in the center of town. Just a few minutes from our house, we eagerly wait for the six o'clock mealtime. All of us wear our new outfits freshly bought for Christmas. I feel rich and important walking through the door. My whole family puts on a charade of wealth as we escort Mom to the table and allow others to care for our coats and belongings.

Apparently tonight marks a change in the family structure because Mark has decided to place the appetizer and drink order—I don't remember being consulted and there's something pathetic about a boy trying to be a man as he orders himself a virgin drink and his mother a glass of wine, but I'll acquiesce and refrain from ruining the evening. I love tonight because there's no item off-limits on the menu. Mom always says tonight we can have anything we want for appetizers, dinner, and dessert.

Once the waitress has taken our complete order, and this time I'm allowed to order my broiled lamb chops on my own, the table quiets quickly as the obligatory chatter over who's having what has passed with the returning of the menus.

"I never asked," Mom breaks the silence, "how was your Christmas at your father's?"

"Good," Layne blurts quickly while Mark swallows his drink hoardingly so that he can reply before me.

"Terrible," Mark proclaims and I can feel a new diatribe coming and I want to avoid it all together so we can have at least one meal where we don't have to pretend to be happy, but I feel that moment slipping away like the last piece of fried calamari on the plate Layne and I shared.

"Oh," Mom says partially surprised, I suppose. I guess she too has become accustomed to all of us saying things were fine and then moving quickly on. But not this time.

"I'm not going up there next year, I hate going. It's a waste of my time and I can't stand looking at Lois, and Dad's so pathetic it makes me sick. How can he be so clueless about everything? I'm never going up there again. EVER!"

"It can't be that bad, I don't hear your brothers complaining," Mom intones.

And now I'm being drawn into a conversation that I want no part of; I can feel my face reddening and the sweat trickles down from my underarms and I wish somebody would say something different.

But Mark continues, "Andrew doesn't have a clue. He's so ignorant and scared to say anything to upset anyone…" Mark's partially right, I am scared to upset people. I don't like to be yelled at and I can't stand watching other people fight. I'm not aggressive, but I'm not ignorant either. "...and Layne's too young to understand."

"I'm not ignorant, I'm just not looking to pick a fight," I toughly reply.

"That's a load of bull. I'm not looking for fights, it's just plain terrible up there and I'm not going to stay quiet about it any longer."

"If Dad gave you a million dollars you'd still say it's awful, you're never happy."

"Shut up, Andrew, everything that comes out of your mouth is so stupid."

It's amazing, the one person I don't like seems to be the only person who can hurt me. I'm used to people insulting me, but I usually don't care. I can't stand Mark, yet his insults are the only ones that hurt me.

"This is embarrassing," Layne chimes in. And he's right; the youngest one in the family speaks with the most sense.

"I'm not going up there and it's final!" Mark declares with a fist on the table as the waitress turns the corner with a tray full of five star meals. She presents the meal to us and we smile, eat, and pretend to be happy.

At 9:45 I'm just about the last one to arrive at Harris's house for the party. His parents are gone in Vermont and he has the house to himself. Inside, I find most of my friends half drunk already. But it doesn't take 15 and 16 year olds too long to get drunk so I know I can catch them quickly. And as shot-gunning beers and shots of tequila begin with my arrival, I know I'll match them soon.

Across the room I see Jennifer; I've had a crush on her since cross country season began in August, but I've been too reticent to talk to her. She's been hanging out with us since school started this year, and I keep telling myself I'm just waiting for the right time. Chris, Mike, and Darrin know all about my feelings for her. I'm sure they've told her, but we pretend like it's all top secret. But I know it's not because I've heard from Lisa that she told her that she really likes me and hopes that I'll ask her out.

So as I play it off like I haven't spotted her yet, I pop my personalized bottle of champagne hoping to get that warm drunk on while I slur to Darrin my master plan of kissing her when the ball drops and allowing that to be my introduction. From there, who knows where we'll go. Darrin pounds my chest then slaps me five to show his approval for my plan. He has my back so I know nothing will fail, I just have to wait until midnight for it all to begin.

Sitting in the orange plush armchair, I just fog in my haze and watch Jennifer from a distance. She's really small and I like that the most about her. Being skinny, I fear being overpowered physically and don't want to be crushed. I think about lying in bed with her and what it would be like to suffocate while making out, even though the mere thought of lying in bed with a girl scares me to death. I wonder if I'll do it right. Not even sex. Even the little things, like kissing and touching. I wish there were someway that I could practice, but that's never going to happen and all of my friends seem so confident about knowing what to do. Of course, I pretend to be the man and tell of all my master plans, but I wonder if their stories are just like mine: lies.

As the hour approaches and everyone seems to be getting themselves nice and ripe drunk for the occasion, I start to make my move. Like a turtle in its most clandestine of moves, I mosey into Jennifer's general area. Her straight blonde hair calling me to her while her rosy cheeks and perfect smile entrance me. I nudge myself next to her in a moment of coincidence. Pretending to be preoccupied by Dick Clark's countdown, I gently bump my hip into hers and try to seem surprised by the 'chance' encounter. Apologizing pathetically, we both strike up trivial conversation. I can feel her heart racing, as she is just as nervous as I am. In my head, I'm concentrating on not saying something stupid while trying to ignore the rings of sweat forming at every pore in my body. I know she likes me and feels the same, yet I cannot calm myself as I stare into her green eyes with a gaze of admiration matched only by her own stare.

10-9 I can hear the count loud and clear from Harris's television as I fumble for Jennifer's hand and hold it tight as the crowd reaches five. Quickly discarding my champagne and taking a long, slow breath I prepare for the moment I've dreamt about for months, yet it seems so far away and I'm scared she'll turn her head the other way when I dive in…

…But she doesn't and I'm surprised by Jennifer's aggressiveness.

Expecting nothing more than a return of my innocent kiss, I find myself tongue and tongue with Jennifer for seemingly minutes in the center of the basement enjoying every last minute of it. Trying to enjoy the moment, my brain gives my body thousands of things to think about and the only one that reaches my consciousness is the amazement that her lips and tongue taste of the sweetest mint despite the numerous drinks that have tried to stale her breath.

As our lips unlock I can feel myself reaching for a breath, but in the most amazing way that I never thought was possible. I look deep into her eyes and find a smile that tells me everything that I've always dreamt about has always been meant to be and now I regret waiting for so long to make it happen. But as I grab her hand and start to lead her upstairs in a flirtatious way that I didn't even know I was a capable of, I feel excitement in my veins tempered only by my own Christian ideals yelling at me to be a good boy mixed with the insecurities that I've never been able to shed about how to please a girl.

And as we stumble into the first open room we can find, it all seems so natural, the more aggressive she becomes, the more aggressive I become and soon I notice that both of our clothes are littering a previously spotless floor. I don't know how far she's willing to go, but I'm certainly willing to find out so long as I can quiet that Sunday school voice which continues to vibrate my skull.

1/1/02

Aching in every morsel that is my body and parched for thirst, I watch Jennifer sleep soundly in the tent I've formed with my arms and elbows around her soft body. I wonder if she'll be happy about the position she's in when she awakens. I remember last night clearly and the feeling left in my mind and body will last a lifetime, yet I long already to feel it again.

As she wakes, I immediately kiss her and massage her body in a boyish attempt at intimacy that she appears to appreciate and we quickly repeat last night's passion almost identically and the feeling during sobriety is even greater than before, and I know this is the girl that I'll forever love.

Moments later we make the bed and clothe ourselves. We go

hand in hand downstairs to greet the morning and our friends with the same secrecy. Some are already up stumbling for food and aspirin while others sleep alone in cold environments and still a few doors remain shut and I wonder if the world behind the door mimicked mine last night, went further, or spiraled into a grand disappointment of frustration.

I don't want to go home, but Jennifer has to and I know I must too if I want to remain in Mom's good graces. I hold Jennifer close to me for one last moment as her ride prepares to drive them home. As the car pulls out of the drive way and passes me on my short jaunt home, I walk on clouds and wonder where we'll go from here.

The door at my house seems heavier than normal, but it doesn't bother me. When Mom asks how my night went, I'll make it sound dull and boring with just a few guys hanging out and she'll see through me even though we'll both pretend not to.

Later, my brothers and I watch football and I want to brag about my night. Layne probably won't feel jealous, but we both know that Mark's night was truly full of just a couple of guys hanging out in boredom. Layne probably "got more than me" and in some ways I'm jealous of my eighth grade brother because nothing scares him and he's the envy of every teen girl in the tri-state area, and I wish I had his smoothness, but I don't. Right now, that doesn't bother me because I have Jennifer and I'm basking in my own afterglow fearing if the phone call I make tonight is too soon, too late, or just right.

1/6/02

School started again today. I don't really mind going to school. It's the one place where I can see all of my friends at once. For the most part my teachers don't bother me. I don't mind going to class and usually like what I'm learning. Even math, which has always been difficult for me, interests me. I can't stand doing homework, which is why I'm writing this journal, rather than finding congruency in triangles using the various theorems we've learned in class. I just have trouble motivating myself to get it done. I'd rather talk to Jennifer on the phone all night and just listen to her stories.

Today during lunch Jennifer and I sat together. Since we don't have any of the same classes, she's a freshman and I'm a sophomore, lunch gives me something to look forward to all morning. Even though many of our friends surround us, we have our own private conversation. We haven't hung out since New Year's, but she wants to do something Friday night and I'm already looking forward to it. Jennifer tells me that it's my job to come up with a date that doesn't involve our parents, which is tough since neither of us drives.

English class follows lunch and Gregg and Harris heckle me all the way down the hallway for the way Jennifer and I smooch before parting ways until practice. Once class begins, the teasing continues. As Mr. Blackwell summarizes *The Scarlet Letter*, Harris chirps his lips at me while pointing at a little sticker on his shirt that says "My name is Jennifer." I laugh while blurting 'shut-up', which draws the attention of Mr. Blackwell. He scolds me for my rudeness and tells me we'll continue this discussion after class. And we do, and I'm quite upset about his discourse. He berates me for my inattentiveness and then lashes into my work quality. He wonders how a kid with such an elaborate vocabulary and keen sense of detail fails to turn in homework and submits writing assignments barely acceptable for an elementary school student. It's true; my work at home lags far behind my work done in class. I tell him that I'll focus more on my homework and I'm sorry for talking.

I'm truly sorry for the talking part, but the homework part is to just get him off my back. I like Mr. Blackwell; he's the only teacher I have who's younger than either of my parents and he seems more like the older brother I want rather than the older brother I'm stuck with. I love English class and read all of the books; it's just answering the redundant guide questions and reader response journals that drives me crazy. I enjoy seminars and actually look forward to the writing assignments–especially about a book that inspires me. But I frustrate him because he knows I've read the book and he can't figure out why I won't do the questions and journals. I want to tell him that his guide questions and journals are inane, but I don't want him to hate me, so I lie and tell him I'll try harder.

Coach Bennett yelled at me throughout the entire indoor track practice today. He'd given us daily workouts to complete over break, of which I'd done none. Doing eight half mile runs nearly bankrupted my entire oxygen supply; luckily I'd barely eaten anything at lunch otherwise it would have been all over the track.

Coach Bennett has never truly liked me and I've always gone back and forth from kissing his ass to hating his guts. During cross country season he called me 'wasted potential' for the entire season because I didn't run enough over the summer. I still made varsity and was better than most of the upperclassmen, but that wasn't good enough for him. He gives me this bullshit line about settling for second when I could've had first. I see his point, but I'm just a sophomore and I know I have plenty of time to prove him wrong. But today I didn't want to hear it from him. I sucked and I knew it. Jennifer tells me not to worry about it at the end of practice, but it's hard. My dad stopped watching my athletics when I stopped playing baseball. He never missed a baseball game growing up. Funny, though, he can never make it to a cross country or track meet, even when they're on Saturdays. Mom hated baseball and rarely came, but that didn't bother me because Dad was always there. Every year she makes it to one cross country meet, one indoor track meet, and one outdoor track meet. Rather than being glad that she's there, I dread the moments because I want to impress her so badly, but I know I won't win so she'll have no clue that finishing 24th out of 77 runners in a cross country meet is still pretty good.

Sometimes I don't even know why I run.

So as I start to feel better with Jennifer saying it'll be alright, Coach Bennett walks past and sees us arm in arm and offers his relationship advice. As if I'm not even there, he says, "You know Jennifer, Andrew only gives fifty percent at track, can you expect any better from him in a relationship?" He smiles and walks away.

I give him the finger as he turns for the next hallway; I think he senses it, but chooses to ignore it as he struts to his teal Dodge Neon.

I ask Jennifer, "What kind of a man drives a teal compact car?"

"A substitute teacher," she replies and we both laugh it off.

After being put down all day by the people who are supposed to encourage me, my mother tops the cake. Because she works late and

Mark forgot to pick me up from practice, I have to walk home. It's my night to cook dinner, even though I've been at school since sunrise and now it's over an hour past sunset and Mark had a long day of jerking off to Internet porn. Mom will be home by seven and dinner must be ready when she comes home; rushing, I spill the garden salad I've made all over the floor and that leaves just pasta and bread for dinner. Throughout the entire meal Mark complains about there not being a salad or enough food as a result.

"Thank your clumsy brother," Mom points at me. I want to spill everything that's left on their plates and scream that I TRIED MY BEST. But they won't care. So I eat silently and none of us even pretend to be happy. Except Layne, who doesn't like salad anyways and tells me as I clean the table that the garlic bread was really good tonight.

So I don't feel like doing my homework because it's past eight and I'm so tired and I have to get up at 5:30 tomorrow and I hate my coach and my family right now. I don't even see the point. I forgot my fucking English notebook in my locker and Mr. Blackwell will yell at me for not doing my English homework after our talk. And I actually meant to do it tonight. I think that maybe I can do it during lunch, but that'll probably upset Jennifer because I won't be spending time with her. And all I want to do is sleep.

I called Jennifer and bemoaned my situation. She listened with a sympathetic ear as I described my inner demons; how I wish myself into a hole never to rise again, to simply hide. She didn't say much after that, and immediately I regretted sharing this with her. Yet another thing to agonize my mind over.

1/10/02

Before I take a shower and get ready to see Jennifer, I just wanted to write. I'm so excited I can hardly contain myself. At seven o'clock we're going to meet downtown and go to dinner and a movie. I feel so grown up. Her parents are going to drop her off so I'll make a point of getting there early. Even though I'll have to walk a mile in the freezing cold from my house, I can't wait to leave.

All day during school she was on my mind. Every class quickly became a daydream of the two of us sharing a meal and holding each other during the movie. I don't know what movie we'll see, but I don't care. She can pick when we get there and I'll enjoy it just because I'm with her. As Mr. Blackwell relived the lusting of Hester Prynne yet again, I guess my subconscious met my conscious and my daydream took a startling turn. Fixating on our date in my dream and Blackwell's repeated use of the words 'lust' and 'sex' crashed somewhere, because a day-dream involving Jennifer and me enveloped my conscience until the shrill sound of the bell startled me back to reality and the realization that I'd just missed an entire lesson.

I must confess, as I prepare for my date, I'm shaking already. Jennifer and I haven't been alone in private since New Year's and I wonder how things will go. We'll be in public and I don't know if we should kiss, hold hands, or walk like friends. I want to be confident and lead, but I don't want to push her away. And the movies will be a whole new problem. It's dark, but everybody will still know what everybody else is doing and making out seems juvenile and holding hands for two hours seems just as silly. Here I am going on the date I've always wanted and I'm so Goddamned nervous that I can't wait for the time to pass. Pathetic.

1/11/02

I have to get up in a few hours for track practice; only Bennett would schedule practice at seven in the morning on a Saturday.

But I can't sleep. I just want to sit up all night and think about Jennifer. We went to the Village for dinner and shared meals. Sometimes when I watch people do that I think of how gross it is and wonder why they'd ever want to share dinner. But now I see why. It just felt right, we had several plates to clutter the table and none of them were hers or mine; they were ours. The eggplant parmesan, penne chicken, and antipasto salad seemed twice as good tonight. When we both reached for the same plate we played war with our forks, laughed, and shrunk beneath the glares of the nearby tables. But we didn't care as we knew they thought of us as just stupid kids making a scene. I don't really remember what we talked about, but it seemed so natural the whole time.

Walking to the theater, I just reached for her arm and we ambled with our arms locked in the cold January air watching our breath drift away towards the streetlights, giving heat to my entire body. Cold was nowhere to be found and my heart ached from the joy of being with my girl.

Jennifer picked some Tom Cruise movie to see that I'd never heard of, but I pretended to be all for it with a passion and earnestness that even surprised me. As Jennifer led me into the theater, she took me to her favorite seat, the back left corner where we had to go backwards just to get to our seast. Only two seats are in the row and nobody from the other aisle could see us. As we sat down, I knew she'd chosen the surreptitious spot on purpose. Perhaps she'd been here before with another guy and remembered the privacy, but I didn't want to think about that.

As soon as we sat down, Jennifer spread the blanket over the two of us. She'd brought it because she said she always gets cold in the movies. I didn't have the guts to tell her that it was probably 80 degrees in the theater. I just pretended to be cold as well.

Once the previews ceased and the lights went out, I soon realized the purpose of the blanket. Slowly, almost like a newborn on his first legs, I felt Jennifer's hand free of my grip, then crawl down my side toward my hip. Instinctively, I tried to mimic her movements and came to a final stop right on the button of her pants. Her choice of loose sweater worked out perfectly as I had nothing tucked to worry about. Not wanting to startle her, but also letting her know I was ready to play, I allowed my index and forefingers to gently massage her bellybutton. As I tickled her, I felt my belt slacken and heard the pop of my jeans being unbuttoned. Beltless as she was, I simply opened her jeans as well. Neither of us had the gall to look at the other, and we both pretended to be fixated on the movie, just in case anyone should turn and look at us.

Two teenagers in a dark movie theater can find all sorts of trouble without anybody ever finding out, I think we both discovered the truth in that serum tonight.

I know you're probably thinking I'm a typical teen male just looking for a girl to take advantage of, but I'm really not. Jennifer is the second girl I've ever kissed in my life. She's the first person I've had any kind of sexual relationship with and it's totally freaking me out. I wasn't prepared for all of this action and I can't believe it's happening so quickly. Lying here in bed, I wonder what God's thinking of me right now. My conscience feels guilty, yet my mind says I've done nothing wrong. I can't talk to my mom about this and I won't talk to Mark about it. I want to talk to my dad, but I'm the same boy who learned to shave from his mom and I don't want to talk on the phone to my dad about sex. I surfed the Internet for information about sex and how to do it, but it always gave me unbelievable porn or advice for girls, which I don't need either. I thought about a book, but I'd be too embarrassed to buy one or check one out from the library. So I guess I'll just learn on my own, wherever that may take me.

1/12/02

I hate Bennett. I come five minutes late for practice and owe him five extra laps. Fucking Shepherd comes ten minutes late and Bennett tells him he's glad he could make it. I run the fucking laps all by myself cursing Bennett and Shepherd the entire time. If I could run a 4:29 mile like Shepherd and be dropped off in a BMW for practice I know I'd be allowed to come and go as I pleased too. I hate Bennett. I really hate Bennett.

1/13/02

It's funny how Sunday mass brings out the worst in all of us. Mass starts at 10:00 so you'd think it would be no problem for the four of use to be ready, especially since we spent years evacuating the house by 7:00. But an hour prior to mass I'm standing in the shower listening to Layne scream about having no clothes to wear while Mom screams at Mark to get up for mass. We're never going to make it and everyone is going to disparage us for coming late.

Yet somehow we manage to slip in just seconds before mass

begins and we elude the preaching eyes of the congregation, but I still feel Someone tapping me on the shoulder, and I'm scared to turn around.

As the priest asks us to call to mind our sins, the tapping I felt has become a tug-o-war between myself and myself. I want to call to mind my indulgences with Jennifer, and how a good Catholic boy would never succumb to such desires before marriage. But I'm not sorry for it, I enjoyed what happened, and I didn't hurt anybody. I guess I always thought a sin was when you hurt somebody else, like adultery, murder, and stealing. But I know I didn't hurt Jennifer and she didn't hurt me. So why do I feel like a dirty sinner in the house of God? I look all around me, I wonder if others feel as I do, or are they all good Catholics just covering up?

And yet Mass can be so beautiful. Every time I think of Christ giving His life for me, I want to cry, and just tell Him thanks, but I know that sounds stupid so I keep it to myself. And the songs are beautiful too. Sometimes I catch myself humming a song at practice or with my friends, and I hope I'm able to quickly repress it before they catch on to the God part.

Fifteen minutes before mass ends, we all wish each other peace. "Peace be with you," must be uttered hundreds of times from scores of lips. The whole idea that we might live in harmony is so cool. But then mass ends and leaving the parking lot becomes a free for all as SUV's driven by newly formed families cut off Charles and Ethel out for their Sunday drive in an oversized Cadillac. Funny, they two just exchanged vows of peace a few moments ago and now their honking horns and flipping each other the bird just to see who can save three seconds leaving mass.

Not that my mother's car is any different. Again, Mark has assumed the leadership role forcing Mom into the passenger seat of her own car. Apparently dad's house and church have assumed the same form as Mark insists that he's never going to this lame-ass church ever again. He praises his newfangled church at college that has so much singing and so many young members. I swear to God he's a genius. It's a miracle that a church on a college campus has a more youthful feel than a church in a rich, suburban, white man's, near retirement community.

"Shocking, isn't it Mark," I joke sarcastically.

"Shut-up you imbecile," Mark tells me. "All I'm saying is that this place could put an insomniac to sleep."

Six days. That's it. Then Mark goes back to college and I will be happier, maybe even not depressed. But I doubt it. Even when Mark's gone, I still have to deal with all of the little things that bother me, especially the feelings that nobody would even notice if I wasn't here. Jennifer makes that feeling go away a lot; I don't have it when I'm with her. But when she's gone, she's all I want and without her my heart burns and I'd do anything to stop that pain, even if that means ceasing to exist. Plus Mark being gone only means the countdown to his return will begin. And with each day the idea of his returning becomes closer and closer to a reality.

And Bennett. God, I hate Bennett.

1/18/02

Because he said he wasn't sure when the next time he'd get to see me run would be, Mark came to my track meet today. I ran a solid leg in the 3200-meter relay, kept my team right in it. Simon ran a great anchor leg and we won the race. Bennett was all smiles and even slapped me five saying, "That's the way to do it!" It felt really good to be congratulated by him, and my brother saw it. I'm not a waste, and I showed it to both of them! I ran the third leg, which is usually the weakest leg of the relay, and I concede that I am one bad race away from being replaced on the relay, but I ran a 2:07 today, which was better than the second leg and by far my best ever.

But all good things come to an end. Usually when the two-mile starts I still feel fresh, but not today. I'm still trying to catch my second wind as the race begins and I struggle to stay up with the lead pack. By the one-mile mark, I'm fading fast and I've resigned myself to finishing in the middle of the pack. As the race draws to a close I can see my time surpassing the 11:20 mark and I haven't been this slow since

November. I try to justify it with the great race I ran earlier in the day and that I haven't fully recovered yet. Which is a good excuse, and I know it. Across the finish line, 8th out of 17 in a race I probably could've finished top four or five.

"Terrible, why even bother Andrew," Bennett greets me at the finish line.

"Sorry coach, I tried."

"That wasn't trying, you were out of the race by the mile mark and never even fought back. See what happens when you don't run over the breaks! God damn it Andrew, when the hell are you ever gonna learn. Go cool down."

"Coach, I never recovered from the 800 earlier."

"If you'd run like you were supposed to have over Christmas break you wouldn't have this problem, Andrew."

"I know, sorry."

"Go cool down."

On my cool down, I see Mark shaking his head at me. He knows I failed, and he's smiling about it. He almost had to congratulate me on my 800, but now he can rub the two-mile in my face. He leaves tomorrow. Just remember that, tomorrow and he'll be gone, now how do I get rid of Bennett?

1/19/02

As Mark packs the car and readies himself for the second semester, I wonder if anybody else is as happy as I am. Mark always says he can't wait to go back, and I can't wait for him to go. Mom seems sad, she's kind of red in the face, but she has a way of creating emotions for the moment. Like a chameleon, I've seen her go from raging bitch to sympathetic friend to devastated sister so quickly that I could swear her head must spin when I'm not looking. I remember several years ago when she was screaming at me for getting in trouble with my friends. The police had knocked on our door and informed her that they'd seen me and my friends ducking into our garage after chucking buckets of stolen apples from the local orchard into one of our "friend's" swimming pool. God did she scream at me. And in the midst of the screaming, our old neighbor called, and suddenly her tone shifted to nostalgia; as I sat in the living room, I could here Mom bragging about Layne being on the honor roll and how well we were all doing and how proud she was of all of us. I guess reality is dependent upon the circumstances created around it.

Anyway, Mark packs our dad's wagon and readies himself for college. I know Mark hates the idea of an eight hour drive with our father, funny, he never wants to see him again, but he'll take advantage of Dad when he's offering to help, especially with rides to college and tuition. As they load the last bag, Mark beams a smile at me and invites me to come and visit him. We both know that won't happen because Mom would never let her 15 year old kid stay on a college campus, and I would never go and visit Mark. But we both pretend to be genuine and both Mom and Dad smile at our "brotherly love."

I watch in apprehension, fearing the car won't start or something drastic will keep Mark here.

And as the loaded down wagon fades down the street, I wait an extra minute to make sure it doesn't reappear in the opposite direction. Adequately satisfied that it won't return, I celebrate up the stairs and scream, "He's gone!"

"Andrew, that's enough, don't talk about your brother like that," Mom scolds.

"Oh Mom you said you couldn't wait to see him go," I antagonize.

"I didn't mean that, just because he can be a little rough around the edges doesn't mean I don't love him and miss him. He's my son and I love him."

And Mom's done it again, managed to make me feel guilty about discarding my brother, but I feel as though a thousand pounds of shackles have been unlocked and my moment of guilt has already passed.

1/25/02

Jennifer's parents had me over for dinner tonight. At school today, Jennifer said her parents wanted to get to know me better. The only other time I'd met them was in the car ride back from the movies. I told my mom and she said next weekend we'd have to have Jennifer and her whole family over. I couldn't tell if Mom was upset that she wasn't invited to dinner and wanted to one up them by having the whole family, or if she genuinely wanted to meet Jennifer's family. Before going over, Mom bought me a plant to give the family as a thank you and welcoming gift. She also reminded me about manners and not embarrassing myself.

Walking through the door, I felt an eerie sense envelop me that I've never quite experienced before. In retrospect, the feeling must have originated from the irony of walking into the Risons' home for the first time hoping to impress them and earn their trust when in reality I only wanted their daughter—I think they sensed that. I fumbled with the plant and speaking and walking and said something stupid about being nice to meet this plant. I think they understood what I was trying to say, so they took the plant appreciatively and invited me in.

The Risons have a beautiful home, much larger and better decorated than my own. I don't know what they do for a living, but judging by their house and cars, something that brings in a lot of money. Jennifer's always told me that she has two younger brothers, but I'd never met them before. She always asks me about my brothers, and I always talk about them. But she never really says much about hers. She told me that she has a younger brother, Aaron, who goes to Eastside Elementary and another brother, Bradley, who's in the seventh grade at Green Hills Middle School.

Following Jennifer and her parents into the kitchen, I wasn't prepared to meet her brothers. Bradley reminds me a lot of Layne, though I don't think they know each other. The middle school where they attend is divided into houses, and despite being just a year apart, the seventh graders and eighth graders virtually never cross paths. But it's Aaron who catches me off guard. He's visibly different, and I can't tell what's wrong with him. I vaguely remember a television show where one of the actors had Downs Syndrome, and I think that's what's wrong with Aaron.

During dinner, I find myself looking in his direction a lot. I'm trying not to stare at him, but it's clear that eating is a great challenge for him, but he's doing it all by himself. I want to ask Jennifer what's wrong with him, but I don't want to be rude or upset her.

Aaron doesn't really say much of anything during dinner except that he wants more mashed potatoes, to which Mr. Rison quickly obliges. Most of the dinner conversation involves Mr. and Mrs. Rison alternating questions shot in my direction. They ask me about school and track, my family and brothers, what I like to do in my spare time, have I started thinking about college and so forth. Finally, I can tell he's been itching to ask it, Mr. Rison interrogates me about my two pierced ears displaying silver hoops on both sides. I notice Mr. Rison's eyebrows skyscraper as I explain that I did it a few months ago because I always wanted to and I thought I'd like it.

Jennifer doesn't allow him to ask a follow up question.

After dinner, Jennifer and I watch a movie in the living room with her parents hanging around 'chatting' in the kitchen. Every twenty minutes or so her mom pops in with a snack or a beverage. Gee, I wonder why.

During a slow part in the movie, I ask Jennifer as kindly as I can about Aaron. She tells me that he's mildly retarded and will probably never be able to live on his own. She says that he was born like that, but her parents insist on sending him to school like any other child. Last year, she says, he played soccer and this year they're going to try to give him piano lessons. I tell her how sorry I feel for him; she just says that it's okay.

Mrs. Rison gives me a ride home. This time I don't know where to sit. When the Risons gave me a ride home from the movies a couple of weeks back, it was easy because her parents were in the front seat and we had only the back to choose from. But this time, Mr. Rison stays home and I dread the decision facing me. Luckily, Mrs. Rison senses it too and tells us to sit in the back while she plays the chauffeur.

My mom waves to Mrs. Rison from the window, but the two still haven't met. I tell Mom all about dinner and the movie and their house. I tell her about how nice the Risons seem, I really do like them.

But mostly I tell Mom about Aaron. And how much it bothers me.

Mom tells me something so gently, that I didn't know it was my mother talking. She tells me that God gives everyone a cross to carry in life. Some people wear theirs on the outside and are easy to see, like Aaron's. Other people have to carry their burdens on the inside. And some share their crosses with others. Mom tells me that God gives us all a cross to carry, but nobody carries a cross that we're not capable of carrying. Just like Jesus carried a cross, so do we. I tell her that Jesus died on His cross. And she reminds me that some people helped Jesus carry his cross while others made it more difficult. She says it's our job as people to help each other carry our crosses.

I'm beginning to understand. I think about my mom. She carries a very heavy cross. She's a single parent working ten and twelve hour days trying to support three kids all by herself. She doesn't have enough time to even think about remarrying or dating. Occasionally, she dates, but once a month isn't really dating. I think about how much of her life is either spent at work, or doing things for others, like grocery shopping, laundry, and cleaning. As I look at her, I want to ask her about her cross, and I start to, but I can tell that she doesn't really want to talk about it. So I ask her about mine.

I ask her if not having a father around is my cross.

She tells me that's up to me to decide.

I don't understand her answer. So I ask her again. This time she explains about how in some ways I'm lucky because I have a nice place to live, food, clothes, a loving mother, and everything I need. But she tells me things aren't everything and a boy should have a father.

"Your father's not a bad man, he loves you guys all very much," Mom concedes.

"I know that, I don't hate him."

"But what he did was run away from his family and leave us behind."

"Mom," I look up, "he told me that if he could do it all again that he would've never left, that he regrets it everyday of his life."

"I know," Mom sighs.

"I believe him, you know, that he's sorry. I forgave him too. Mark hasn't. And that kills him even more. I don't expect you to forgive him, and I think he knows you won't, but I forgive him. People make mistakes. You taught me that."

"I forgave your father long ago. It wasn't just him; we were having a lot of problems. He knows we don't have a lot and sometimes he puts extra in the support checks to help out. I don't love him anymore, and it certainly hasn't been easy."

"Mom, it's your cross."

"Yes, honey, it is."

"Why doesn't Mark forgive him?"

"Because Mark remembers what it was like to have a family. He remembers your father coming home from work and he remembers family dinners and holidays. You and Layne were too young to remember that, so it never really hurt you as much, you've never known it any other way. Mark blames a lot on your father, but someday he'll realize that a lot of people have it a whole lot worse than him."

"Like Aaron," I suggest.

"Maybe. If Aaron's lucky, things might not be too bad. I work with adults like Aaron all of the time. Some have great support and many friends. Others don't and their lives are heart wrenching."

"Mom, why do people hurt each other?"

"Go to bed honey, I love you."

"I love you too. Thanks Mom."

"Andrew," Mom beckons, as I'm half way up the stairs, "the next time you want to know why people hurt each other, think of the way you and Mark act towards each other. Remember how happy you were when he left?"

"Mom, he doesn't know that, he never saw me smile or anything, we shook hands and he invited me down to see him, remember?"

"It's not him you hurt, it was me. I thought I taught you to love your brother."

I nod my head in agreement with her and slowly climb up the rest of the stairs. It never occurred to me that I was hurting her by picking on Mark. Maybe I answered my own question. We don't intend to hurt…ourselves, each other…we just do.

1/28/02

Report cards were distributed today at school, here's a copy of mine:

Class/Teacher	Q1	Q2	Ex	Sem	Comments
Geometry J. Reynolds	C	C	D	C	Poor test scores
Biology R. Fitzpatrick	C	C	C	C	Fails to complete home-work
English D. Blackwell	C	B	A	B	Works below ability
European History J. Gephen	B	C	B	B	
Spanish II S. Daly	C	C	C	C	Fails to complete home-work
Health S. Briben	C	C	B	C	Fails to complete home-work
Keyboarding E. Jacobson	B	B	C	B	

I quickly scanned the column marked Q2 because I know that only quarter grades figure into academic eligibility and since this is the end of the second quarter, only that column means anything to me. I add the grades and see that I've easily cleared a 2.0 and I'll be able to run track no questions asked. Mom will be mad about the D on the exam for Geometry, but I had nothing lower than a C for the semester so all will be well at home. The comments I'll have to explain, but that won't take but a second, I figure.

At track practice we have to show our report cards to one of the coaches; shocking, Bennett immediately asks to see mine. I think he hopes that I haven't cleared a 2.0, but with 5 C's and 2 B's I'm coasting at a 2.3 or something.

Bennett glares at the report card, then me, "Get in hallway, NOW!"

I'm not quite sure what I did, but I'm out of the team room and sitting on the hard tile floor for several minutes before the door opens. I look up pleadingly to the team being dismissed for warm-ups. No one says a word to me, and I sit laconic and motionless.

"Andrew, get in here," Bennett commands from the hallway.

I reluctantly enter the room asking, "What's wrong coach?"

"Is this all a game to you?"

"No," I answer confusedly for I don't know what 'this' is referring to and I want to clarify his indefinite pronoun with faulty modification.

Tossing my report card at me, Bennett screams, "You're the smartest fucking kid on this team and you bring this piece of shit home to your parents?"

"Mom."

"What?"

"I said mom, I don't live with my dad; he'll probably only hear about my report card; he'll never see it."

"And what will your mom say?"

I don't like the way Bennett is questioning me, and I want to tell him to fuck-off and that my family is none of his business, but I sense this situation is pretty bad and I don't want to irritate him any further.

"She'll say I could've done better, but nothing below a C is fine."

"Bullshit."

"Excuse me, coach?"

"Your mom works what 12 hours a day? And she raises you all by herself, and all you can do is this? That's bullshit. If you don't make honor roll next quarter you're off the team, no spring track."

"You can't do that, all I need is a 2.0"

"I can cut whoever I want, you don't have to make the team Andrew."

By the time Bennett's dismissed me, the team has already finished their three warm-up laps and he makes me run my three plus three more for missing the first three. I know he's doing it to me on purpose. And he stares me down the entire time with an impish smirk on his face. As I finish the laps, he mysteriously leaves practice for several minutes, and though I'd normally be relieved by his absences, this time I feel sick to my stomach.

Rarely does Mom pick me up from practice, usually I either have to bum rides with a friend or walk, but today she's waiting for me at the curb. As I hop into the car, her humor seems quite cantankerous.

"Hey Mom, what's up?

"Not your grades, son," Mom so cleverly replies.

"What are you talking about?"

"Mr. Bennett called me at work and told me how you're doing poorly in your classes. He read me the comments off your report card and you could have done better in almost every class."

"Mom, I got nothing below a "C" damn it!"

"I work too hard for you to be average. There's going to be no going out until I see your homework done. Just wait 'til I tell your father."

"That's not fair. He's not here to do anything about it. You can do what you want to me, but I'm not doing what he says."

"Fine, Andrew, when we get home you can just sit in your room and do your homework. No phone, no television, no friends."

After staring at the walls for twenty minutes or so and seeing that Mom's serious, I start to look at my Geometry book. I want to call Jennifer, but Mom's got my phone and I sure as hell don't feel like proving the congruency of triangles based on the multiple theorems and proofs...who gives a damn about side-angle-side?

Mom took my stereo, but she didn't take my guitar. I start strumming a song by Grant Lee Buffalo, you've probably never heard of it, the singer repeats "Honey don't think you're liable to figure me out" several times. It's the only part of the song I play. I sing it quietly to myself, I am, after all, the only person who sounds bad to himself while singing in the shower and I'm self conscious about humming a tune anywhere. Grant Lee Buffalo is not Emo, but this song is. And I feel like that right now. I break into several tunes by the Samples before I settle on "A Slow Motion Crash." I like this one the best right now because I really feel like my life is slowly crashing, and I cannot stop it. Mom didn't show me any passion when I told her that I scored an A on my first essay of the semester for Blackwell. It was a really good essay too. I think you'd like it. It was all about the greatest sinners in *The Scarlet Letter* were the townspeople and not Hester and Dimmesdale. But Mom doesn't like talking about sinners so she told me that she'd read the essay some other time. She still hasn't read it. But apparently she read my report card.

"I told you to do your homework!" Mom screams from the hallway, "put that guitar away now!"

"I'm practicing for guitar class," I lie, "I'm supposed to practice for 45 minutes a day."

"You don't have guitar class."

So I play the strings softer and hope that she can't hear them and yet all I want to do is scream lines from songs that mean nothing to her, but everything to me.

And that's just what I do; Mom tells me to shut up. So I do, and I sit staring at my wall drawing only one conclusion...this is all

Bennett's fault.

1/29/02

School sucked today. Jennifer cried to me about how I don't love her because I didn't call her last night. I tried to tell her what happened and how I lost my phone privileges, but she seems to think I should've found a way to call her. She wouldn't come to lunch; she ate in the bathroom with her friend Lisa. And Bennett pretended I didn't exist at practice today, which I guess would normally be a good thing because he didn't yell at me once, didn't talk to me once, didn't correct me once, didn't coach me once. But every time he was near me he made damn sure to praise the person standing next to me. *The slow motion crash is speeding up.*

1/30/02

I just snuck back into my bedroom. I waited until everybody was asleep, tiptoed downstairs, and called Jennifer. It was 1:20 in the morning, but she needed to know that I'm miserable with her mad at me and I really love her. She needed to know that I've stayed up all night just to talk to her, even if she's mad at me.

She was sleeping and was groggy; perhaps that's why she allowed me to talk. I was finally able to explain what happened last night about my grades and losing all of my privileges. She didn't really respond, so I tried to make her laugh by saying that I ate dinner in the bathroom tonight so that I could share something with her. She laughed really hard when I said that, even though I lied, but I knew that we were going to be alright. We talked until past three, and I know I'm going to be exhausted at school and practice, but none of that matters. Jennifer and I are going to be alright.

2/1/02

After class I told Blackwell that I was grounded for my grades and would be sitting home all weekend. I asked for a book to read. He gave me *The Giver* by Lois Lowry and told me to read it by Monday. You've probably heard of this book, its won a lot of awards, it says so on the cover itself. He told me it would make me a more sensitive person and that it would help me out. He says he only gives it to students who can benefit from it and who are special. He says that I'll find out why when I read it. Now I'm excited about reading the book, but then again, I am grounded and Jennifer will be hanging out with everyone, but me, and I'll be reading alone in my room, what a dork!

2/4/02

I came in to school early today to talk all about the book with Blackwell, but he didn't arrive until five minutes before the bell rang so he told me to come at lunch or after school. I have practice after school and I haven't pissed Bennett off for a full week and I don't want to start by being late. But the only time I really get to see Jennifer is at lunch and I know she'll be destroyed if I miss lunch after being grounded all weekend. I try to explain this to Blackwell and ask him if we could talk tomorrow morning or during class one day. But he just scowled at me and said lunch or after school.

My first instinct was to blow Blackwell off—not show up to either meeting. But he'd picked that book just for me and it had moved me in so many ways that I wanted to tell him all about it. Missing track practice certainly wasn't an option; I'd be killed for that. So Jennifer would have to be sacrificed, and I would talk sweetly to her at practice and explain the whole situation to her, and everything would be alright.

Blackwell barely said a word about the book at lunch. He kept asking me questions like "How are you different than your peers" or "What are the characteristics of a leader?" I tried to tie all of my answers into *The Giver* and point out how I was just like Jonas, and he was different and he was a leader. But every time I tried to relate to the book, Blackwell kept cutting me off and saying we're not talking about the book, we're talking about you.

Just as lunch was nearing its conclusion, he finally spoke. Blackwell told me that I was Jonas for everything that I had said to describe myself. But he said I wasn't behaving like him. He said you and Jonas are both different and have all of the characteristics of a leader, but Jonas leads while you follow.

The bell rang, and I was left to ponder Blackwell's words, "Jonas leads while you follow." But whom do I follow?

On time for practice and Bennett out of my ear, though Jennifer was quick to take his place for missing our usual lunch date. I didn't want to talk about that and kept trying to focus our conversation about the book and my conversation with Blackwell. I think she could tell that I was genuinely moved and all of her complaints acquiesced immediately as I retold the whole lunch story. I concluded with Blackwell's last line about Jonas leading and me following and how I was still trying to figure out what he meant by that.

"He's right," was all she said and then she ran off to join the distance girls while I was left standing alone, falling behind the distance boys.

2/15/02

Mom's actually being way cooler than I ever though she would be. My grounding doesn't end until the next report card at the beginning of April, but she's letting me go out with Jennifer tonight to celebrate Valentine's Day, a day belated of course.

It's been over two weeks since I've been allowed out and I haven't seen Jennifer at all, I barely know what to do or where to take her. In the town center there's an arcade, sort of like Chuck E Cheeze's, but not so corny. It's a great time because we can be alone when we want and just hang out, but we can also see our friends, which is nice for me since I haven't hung out with anybody since Bennett got me grounded; I hate him.

The pit of plastic balls enchants both Jennifer and me. After playfully jumping around and tossing balls off of each other's forehead, we bury ourselves in the rainbow colors and kiss in playful bliss. I can hear the sounds of the outside world just above the protective seal of the balls, which we both laugh over, and it feels so good just to be close to her, and to be able to smile and have a good time and know that everything is alright, and we don't have to be pretend to be happy.

Before we emerge from the balls to rejoin our friends, I tell her that I love her and give her a ruby red heart and chain from my pocket. Shocked, she hits me and says that we agreed not to exchange gifts. I sheepishly smile and tell her that being with her tonight was the only gift I needed. I know that was a horrible cliche, but in my heart, it is true. Jennifer looks at me with a twinkle in her eye that I know means she's been touched, but crying in public is out of the question; she kisses me on my lips and says she loves me, adorns her new charm, raps her arm around my wrist, then drags me out of the ball pit and back into reality.

Mom picks me up, and it dawns on me that she was alone for Valentine's Day again, and it probably burned of loneliness on her insides. I know why she let me off grounding for one night. Perhaps Mom isn't as out of touch as I'd like to think she is. Someday, I'm going to make sure that Mom is really happy; I just don't know how, yet.

2/22/02

I'm still grounded, but tonight I went with Mom to her company's annual spaghetti dinner. Mom is a social worker and she works with people who have developmental disabilities. Walking into the banquet hall where the festivities will take place, I notice that Mom is a hero to many. So many of the men, women, and children suffering from mental handicaps rush to embrace Mom. They hug her and welcome her with open arms. She smiles and blushes from eye to eye, then introduces me to everyone. Immediately I'm made to feel welcomed as if I'm Hollywood's newest star.

Dinner is somewhat adventurous, a few spilt salads, over boiling pots, and mismanaged vats of sauce add unneeded steam and confusion to the kitchen. Yet the diners in the hall will never know. A buffet line offering spaghetti, meatballs, Italian sausage, marinara, a plethora of sauces, bread, salad, beverages, and dessert is constantly in need of replenishment. Many local politicians, businessmen, and community members have paid ten dollars each to show their support. Mom never stops. She greets local dignitaries at the door, checks in on the kitchen, and busses tables with a smile on her face. Tonight I'm her runner. Whenever a bowl runs low, it's my job to refill it. One trip for spaghetti, the next for Parmesan cheese and napkins. As the evening draws to a close, we bus the last table and enjoy the leftovers of a fine meal. As we dine, Mom serves as the master of ceremonies for the silent auction. She raffles off gift certificates to various stores, restaurants, and services—all donated, of course, to help those in need.

As we drive home with a few leftovers, Mom is clearly tired, but also proud. Perhaps even of me. I couldn't help but notice how she smiled every time she introduced me, and many of her coworkers seemed to know me already…does Mom really talk about me at work? At home, while I check the messages, Mom throws the leftovers in the microwave and I call to her about how could she be hungry again already? But Mom hasn't eaten at all, she spent almost six hours on a Friday night dining and pleasing everyone but herself.

I feel bad that Mom will eat all alone, so I join her at the table and tell her with complete honesty that I truly enjoyed tonight. I told her I liked her coworkers and how nice so many of the mentally challenged people were.

"Now you know why I don't like it when you and your brothers call each other retards," she instructs.

"Huh?"

"You know, putting each other down. You say it like it's a disgrace or a bad thing. But as you saw tonight, they don't have a mean bone in their bodies. They loved you and they would do anything for me. It's not their fault that they don't possess the same mental strengths that you and I do."

"Oh," I'm understanding her drift now, "Sorry Mom, I won't call people retards anymore. I'm sorry."

"And now you know why you're grounded. You have a gift to be great and God has blessed you in so many ways. And you waste it by screwing around, partying with your friends, and not caring. And I'm working twelve hours everyday and you can't see why I love you so much and why you doing well is so important to me."

"Mom, I didn't want to be lectured tonight. I realized that tonight without you telling me."

"I'm not lecturing you, Andrew. But you need to keep your priorities in line. I work too hard and love you too much to watch you fail."

Yeah, she does work too hard and I know she loves me, but I don't think she understands what I'm going through at school and how Bennett hates me and how Jennifer is always so lonely because I'm not there.

2/26/02

During Blackwell's lecture about how rites of passage intertwined into the story of *Huckleberry Finn*, I found myself bored to tears. As always, I read the book, and now I religiously do the guide questions. It's not that I really want to do the guide questions, but if I have any chance of ever getting off being grounded, I'd better do them and have a picture perfect report card. Anyway, I hate this book. It's so boring. I can't believe Mark Twain is so famous. But he is a Connecticut hero (or Yankee, whatever) with the whole house deal thing on the River and all of our English teachers seem to break into rhythmic orgasms at the mere mention of his name. So as Blackwell trudges on…and on…and on…I drift away…away…aw…

…until the door gently opens and its motion interrupts my blank stare at the board coupled with thoughts of kissing Jennifer on her sweet lips. Bennett! What's he doing here? He leaves the door ajar behind him and stands in the back of the room. I pretend he's not there. But as Blackwell hands out an assignment asking us to write about a rite of passage in our own lives, a palpable sense of dread encompasses my entire being. While the class writes, I break into goose bumps and cold sweats while the two of them covertly converse in the back of the room. Twice I lip read my name off of Bennett's lips and I can feel their eyes piercing my skin and I know this can't be good.

Once Bennett mercifully leaves the class, I find myself partially relieved, but concentrating on Blackwell's assignment is still impossible. I barely finish before the bell and as I turn in my paper Blackwell asks me to stay behind.

"Coach Bennett was asking about you Andrew."

"Oh, really, what'd he want," I pretend to be surprised and totally unaware of his previous presence in the classroom.

"To see how you're doing, making sure you're doing your homework and that your grades are strong. He says you have a lot of potential as a runner and he's just making sure you're keeping up the student part too."

"Oh, yeah," I'm a little disturbed by Bennett's involvement in my school life, but I don't want to turn this conversation into a bashing, so I say as little as possible.

"He really cares about you," Blackwell concludes and I decide my best course of action is to remain silent and stand nodding my head in partial agreement. "Andrew," Blackwell continues, "your next book is *The Basketball Diaries* by Jim Carroll. Have it read by the end of next week and we'll talk about it at lunch on that Friday. Here."

On my way out of Blackwell's class, I'm a little lost on his selection. I don't really like basketball and I didn't know I had joined the book of the month club. But I'm honored that he picked me and I'm still grounded so the added reading won't be any burden at all.

3/2/02

Jim Carroll jerked off on top of a New York City apartment building under the stars all alone at night when he was in high school. And I thought this book was going to be about basketball. In the spirit of the book, I slipped out of my house tonight and landed at Harris' party.

On my way to Harris' house, I couldn't escape the thought of stars. Jim Carroll's escapades partially ruined the pureness I'd always associated with stars. Many nights I would lie in my yard waiting for a star to shoot across the darkened sky or simply try to form my own constellations among clusters of dancing stars. But not now; I look up at the sky and masturbation–somebody else masturbating–invades my thoughts and ruptures the solemnity of the gazing. And in an even more twisted outcome, I desire to try it, or maybe even with Jennifer.

I failed to account for the fact that slipping into my house would be much harder than slipping out. By the time I decided to leave for home, it was brutally cold and I was brutally drunk. I decided that walking was out of the question and called for a ride home. My town, has decided that an anonymous program should exist allowing teenagers to find a safe ride home. In theory, this cuts down on drunk drivers. In my case, this simply provides me with a quicker ride home.

After a seemingly two second stroll through town–I took a nap in the car, I find myself fumbling with the basement window trying to surreptitiously land myself inside my own home. I failed to realize how hard it would be to sneak into my house when I was drunk and feared that I would wake Mom, thus killing my buzz while prolonging my grounding. Luckily, Mom is a sound sleeper and despite my miscues, I land in bed without her noticing my absence nor my graceless return.

3/8/02

At lunch, it was time to discuss *The Basketball Diaries* with Blackwell. I'm really not sure at all why he had me read this book. The main character basically throws away a basketball scholarship on drugs. Almost the entire book involves him being high, searching for a high, or recovering from a bad experience.

In a rare moment of confidence, I decide to strike up the conversation with Blackwell rather than having him direct its course. "Why'd you have me read this book," I blurt out to start the discourse.

"Why do you think I asked you to read it?" he responds.

I look at him without responding, I half expected him to answer my question with another one, but I still hadn't conjured up a response. So I pretend he didn't ask me that question at all and break into a deep-breathed synopsis of the plot. I focus largely on the drug abuse, sex, and partying hoping to get a rise out of Blackwell. I have a feeling that I'm focusing on the very parts that I was supposed to "see through and past." That beyond the indiscretions was a powerful message unraveling before my very eyes and I, Andrew, as Blackwell's prodigy or whatever the hell he thought I was to him, had seen through and found the greater meaning. But here I was, letting him down before his very eyes revealing myself to be nothing more than a run of the mill teenager delivering the adolescent message and Blackwell had failed to see me for who I was, just another kid.

"Precisely," Blackwell nods as I finish my plot overview and suddenly I'm stunned again. Was that the whole point, to have me read about partying and drug abuse and failure?

"So what's the point?"

"The point, Andrew, is that you're heading down the same path."

"What, no I'm not!" I shout in reply. I'm truly offended by Blackwell's assessment of me. So much for Blackwell having a high opinion of me and I want to walk out of his room and tell him off, but that will only justify his beliefs.

“Listen to me, everyday I watch you walk into my classroom with a chip on your shoulder. You don’t care about what anybody says. You do what you want when you want, like my homework. You don’t respect your teachers, parents, or coaches. And do you think I don’t know what you’re doing on weekends?”

“I’m grounded right now.”

“Don’t interrupt me. I know who your friends are and what they do. And I know you’re right there with them. Bennett sees you’ve got potential and ability and you hate him for pushing you to be successful. You resent your teachers for calling your house for having C’s because they know you’re capable of so much better. You don’t care about a damn thing. Remember Jim, he was the main character, remember him sleeping in class, sneaking out of his house, blowing his coaches off, partying when he felt like it? You remember where he ended up, nearly dead and a wasted scholarship. Remember that? That’s where you’re going.”

Somewhere during Blackwell’s diatribe his tone shifted from angry and bitter to pleading and concerned. And though I wanted to scream at him and tell him he was wrong, I also wanted to hug him and tell him that it wasn’t going to be like that. And perhaps worst of all the only thought running through my head was how I snuck out of my house last weekend to go to a party because I really wanted to get drunk with my friends. So I did nothing except sit there with my head down waiting for him to say something. But he didn’t. Blackwell just left the room with me sitting there and the book still in my hands. I hadn’t even taken a bite of my lunch yet, but I wasn’t hungry. I wanted to scream and throw the desks because I couldn’t handle thinking about all of this right now. I wanted to run and tell Jennifer, but I had no where I could take her and cry in her arms without someone being there to laugh or make a joke about us, and I couldn’t stand to hear a joke right now. I wanted to go home and leave school, but that would just make Blackwell seem right and his words had no power on me, that I was a failure and that I was cutting school just two minutes after he told me I was a failure. So I put my head down and let my eyes close and well with tears waiting for lunch to end. And as the bell rang, it dawned on me that I had nowhere to go for I had Blackwell's class immediately after lunch. And as he opened the door and saw me still sitting at my desk with the remnants of tears in my eyes, I was shocked that he pretended nothing had happened.

"Good afternoon, Andrew," was all he said, just like any other day, as if what just happened a few minutes ago had never really happened at all. And I sat through class just staring at him even more confused.

"It's not going to be like that," I told Blackwell as I left the room.

"We'll see," and he patted my back and I heard the noises of the hallway as if it were the very first time.

3/15/02

Today is the first day of outdoor track practice. Our indoor season ended at the end of February and usually the two or three weeks between seasons is a time of atrophy and decadence. But not this time. I took the first two days off to rest and heal, but I've been running everyday for the past two weeks. I can't wait to show off my progress as the others lag behind. Bennett may actually be impressed.

And today we shoveled the track. Figures. I should've realized this would happen given the foot of snow that fell just two days ago. Spring in New England simply means two more months of winter. There weren't enough snow shovels to go around, but Bennett made sure there was one for me. Those without snow shovels had the back breaking task of counting equipment–blocks, shot puts, discuses, etc.– while my back actually broke.

Once the track was clear, we were all sent home and most of the team darted for their cars, but not me. I simply ran lap after lap around the freshly cleared track. Bennett stayed and watched for a second, shook his head, and left me around lap two. Twenty-two laps later I left. Little did I know that Bennett had watched the entire performance from his car. As I sauntered towards the school, he simply gave me a thumbs up and drove away.

Jennifer's birthday is tomorrow and I've been racking my brain for days trying to conceive the perfect gift. Every time I go to a store I stare blankly at the shelves convincing myself that she'll hate whatever contraption I'm holding in my hand. I would love to be able to make her something special, but I have the creativity of a monotone guitar and couldn't think of a good idea that didn't end with me proclaiming my own stupidity.

Something simple, my mother suggests. But I want to impress her and simplicity isn't the answer. Mom reminds me that it's the thought that counts, but that's just an excuse for a terrible gift and I don't want to mess this up.

Finally, I remember that purple is Jennifer's favorite color and I already know the theme...all things purple–purple flowers, purple lollipops, purple, shit, I'm running out of purple things. But then I got it, me, in purple. I find all of the purple dye I can and ruin a perfectly good white t-shirt, but it's purple now. Next, I ruin my socks and boxers, and finally the grayish sweat pants that I haven't worn in years. I even buy hair dye and make my scalp cringe with a burning feeling as the dye does it job. I am Barney on crack.

Sometimes I'm amazed at just how cool my mom really is. In the middle of the dying craze, Mom absconded (hey, I just used a really cool word that I learned in class yesterday) from her own house only to arrive several minutes later with a small box and a demand that I open it at once. Inside, I find a beautiful amethyst pendant on a gold chain. She tells me to give it to Jennifer. I search my pockets for all the spare change and crinkled bills I can find after my purple dye spree, but all I can find is $7.42. I have a feeling the chain and pendant cost more than that and I have no way to pay mom for it. Might I add, that part of me is a little peeved because I don't have this kind of money and I don't want to shell out the dough. But my mom just stands there laughing at me as my purple hands start to turn the money some funky color that could send me to prison for counterfeiting. She tells me that I don't have to pay her for it. And in a moment of mother-son love, she says she's proud of me and all my hard work lately and to think of it as a reward for a job well done.

3/16/02

Family birthday parties suck.

I show up in my party purple and Jennifer's parents give me the evilest eye that ever existed. Jennifer bursts out laughing at the sight of me, but immediately recognizes the thought–I guess that means she doesn't like my appearance. Little did I know that the family birthday dinner was going to be at some posh New Haven restaurant. Who even knew that New Haven had nice places. I've always heard New Haven looked better in the dark and strangers shudder when I tell them I'm from New Haven. They give a forgiving smile when I tell them near New Haven, not the actual city. Anyway, my purple hair, t-shirt, socks, and sweats are quite a site indeed. At least my hiking boots are still brown. I feel like an imbecile at dinner, and to say the least I think I embarrassed more than just myself. The worst of it is meeting Jennifer's grandparents, aunts, uncles, and cousins for the first time. Nothing like making a good first impression.

As dinner progresses and my shame escalates, I notice little purple drops sliding down my cheeks, neck, and forehead. Great! I'm sweating purple hair dye all over the place.

Mercifully, dessert arrives, complete with trick candles and a purple cake–hey I'm not the only creative one. So one by one Jennifer opens presents from her family. I sit there ooing and aahing like a hyena. Secretly, though, as Jennifer unwraps a used CD from her cousin, a hideous sweater from her grandparents, and some kind of keepsake from her parents that I still haven't been able to identify yet, I smile at the knowledge that my gifts will kick all of their gifts' assess. Eventually, she reaches for the paper bag containing the fruits of my labors. First, she sees the purple flowers, I think they're lilies or orchids or something, all I know is that they're flowers and she likes them. Next comes the purple plant, they too are either orchids or whatever; I had stopped listening to the florist once I figured out I could afford them. The lollipops get a laugh from everyone, and a stern warning from her father about rotting teeth. Finally, the pendant. Score! I think she wants to kiss me, but is scared to do so in front of the whole family. However, Jennifer's bright red (not purple) cheeks radiate the darkening air around the table and she immediately clasps the chain around her neck.

A few seconds later she does kiss me on the cheek and grabs my hand for everyone to see. And as if reality finally set in on Jennifer's mother, she proclaims that everything I gave to her daughter was purple, which is of course, Jennifer's favorite color. And to top the idiocy of the moment, Grandma's moment of clarity breaks in with the notion as to why I'm dressed in all purple.

Suddenly I'm not an imbecile.

I'm still an embarrassment, however.

I thought I'd be invited back home to hang with Jennifer and her family, but to no avail. Without even asking, Mr. Rison simply drops me at my doorstep. I thank him for the meal and wish Jennifer a happy birthday. Mr. Rison doesn't let Jennifer reply, rather he tells me to shower and throw away those silly purple clothes. I give him a fake smile as Jennifer tells him to stop it.

Mom asks me about how the pendant went over. I just kiss her and say thank you before I sprint for the shower desperate to regain my manhood.

It was really cool watching all of the purple swirl its way down the drain.

3/19/02

I haven't had the sickening depressed feeling that makes me not want to exist anymore for no particular reason for a couple of weeks now. In fact, I haven't even thought about hiding in a hole or simply disappearing.

But today it wouldn't go away.

Jennifer didn't want to hear about it. She said last time that I told her about this, that it scared her so much that she couldn't sleep. So I didn't talk to her about this anymore. In fact, we just stopped talking.

3/20/02

Jennifer dumped me today.

The feeling is still here.

Just a little worse.

And Jennifer said it was because I was always depressed. I hadn't been depressed in a while, except for yesterday and today. So she waits until I'm depressed to dump me. This ought to make me feel better.

I stared at her during warm ups and drills at track practice looking to see just where the horns sprouted from on her head.

I ran forever today. Practice ended, but I just kept running. It made me feel a little better.

3/22/02

I've decided to stop feeling sorry for myself and to be just plain normal. No more sickly looking, depressed Andrew. It's time to go back to that happy go lucky kid of a few weeks back.

So I go to Blackwell and ask him for a new book to read. See, the problem is that I want something to take my mind off of everything. And I know that the weekend is here and most of my friends will be pushing pills and slugging beers. I don't want that. Which is weird because for a while now my weekends have been consumed either by Jennifer or being grounded. So when Chris and Harris bombarded me with the party plans for the weekend, I initially felt excited. But then I remembered all of the feelings of loneliness that seem to take a death grip on my emotions when I drink. Not to mention the morning after hangovers. And for some reason I want to feel good on Saturday morning for track practice. I'm in shape and probably looking the best of any distance runner on the team. Not that Bennett has complimented me or anything, but he hasn't said anything to me. How can he, his protégée, Shepherd, pulled up lame and the rest of the team is still working off bouts of inactivity. And I don't want to blow it when things are going well.

But back to Blackwell. He wants to talk, which sort of bothers me.

"Andrew, you haven't been yourself this week," he begins. I'm not shocked that he noticed, however, he is the only one to notice. My family, after all, well, Mom's been at work, and it's not a random Saturday so dad's no where to be seen, so how would they notice?

"Jennifer dumped me, and I don't know, I just haven't felt normal," I'm surprised by my candor, apparently I did want to talk about it.

"Normal?"

"You know, not myself."

"Oh," Blackwell slurs, and I can tell that something I've said has struck a nerve with him. I think he wants me to elaborate, but I'm not sure if I want to.

"Well, Andrew, we all go through times when things bother us. Don't be afraid to talk about them. People have feelings, and sometimes our feelings get hurt. But don't allow the hurt and pain to define you."

"What do you mean?" I ask, partially following his drift.

"It's easy to work hard when things are going well. But it's when life has you down that truly defines who you are as a person. So when you don't feel like yourself, accept it, work through it, and come out of it even stronger."

"Ok."

"So what is it that you really want to do this weekend?"

"I don't know, I want to read a book so I don't get wasted with my friends and get my ass kicked at practice tomorrow."

"Then read a book," says Blackwell.

"That's why I came here," I chortle at him.

"Right, but don't read while you feel sorry for yourself. Only read when you want to. And when that time comes you'll have this book to read."

"Thanks," I mutter as I peruse the cover of *This Boy's Life* by Tobias Wolff; I can see the message unfolding simply by reading the title. As I wander down the hall toward practice, I look forward to reading the book, and I know Blackwell's right.

Quickly, I dart back down the hall; there was something I wanted to say to Blackwell, but I forgot to say it. I burst back into his room and simply say, "It's not going to be like that; have a good weekend Mr. Blackwell."

As I start my return sprint down the same hall, I can hear him reply with a genuine "you too."

3/23/02

I don't think I've really told you much about my small New England town. I live in Connecticut, right on Long Island Sound. It's a very wealthy community, though my family is far from wealthy, in fact, we're probably one of the poorest families in town, though we are by no means poor. Anyway, the southern border is Long Island Sound and several miles of beaches are meticulously maintained by either the town itself or the private residences that somehow convinced the government that water and sand could in fact be privatized, but I guess that's the history of America. The biggest beach in town is public and we all hangout there in the summer. Beach volleyball, sailing, basketball, sand fights, and dodge the jellyfish are popular summertime activities. I pride myself on my tan and refuse to use sun screen, my Italian skin protects me.

The east and west borders are two rivers, well, though they're by no means mighty, they do the trick for lazy summer days, reed gazing, and canoeing. The north border is just some line drawn hundreds of years ago. But it's the farther north you travel that seems to find the most interest among us. Life is centered around the beach. Downtown sits just a few blocks from the shore; mom and pop stores surrounded by chain supermarkets and convenience stores. A two play cinema surrounded by coffee shops bearing national resemblance. And, of course, in all New England towns there must be a town green, a meeting room, church, school, and rail depot; our town is no different. But as you travel the two laner north, neighborhoods become more spread out and trees more dense. And as you approach the east and west borders, the farther north you go, the closer you become to no one. Most of the woodlands have no marked trails and little streams jetty off of the small rivers. A few clearings in the woods are barely noticeable amongst the canopy of trees. These hideouts serve as refuge for many of the local teenagers on Friday and Saturday nights when mom and dad refuse to go away for the weekend. It doesn't really matter how cold it gets in the winter, a blazing fire is easy to start as wood is abundant, no one will miss it, and well made tents accompanied by sub-zero sleeping bags keeps everyone warm at night.

I remember the first time I went camping like this. I was in the eighth grade and scared to tell my mom I was going camping with some friends in the woods. I told her it was right in the backyard of one of my friend's house to make it sound supervised. Though she wondered why we picked December, she thought it was a great idea and a productive way to spend a weekend.

She had no clue of the debauchery we planned. While we smoked and drank our brains away, she envisioned us chopping down wood, telling campfire stories, and cooking over an open flame.

Ever since then, I went camping a lot more. The smell of campfire plus the expectation that we stayed up late telling ghost stories always hid my true stench and hangover. What a perfect cover.

My town sits twenty five minutes, seventeen miles, from the city of New Haven. Three towns buffer my town from New Haven. As you head west towards Elm city, each town becomes a bit seedier. The town to my immediate west, ironically bordered by the East River–so I guess it's east to them, is similar to my town, just not quite as nice; and even the next town after it is acceptable. But the town right next to New Haven is where it all falls apart, affectionately known as Staven, instead of East Haven. Staven is blue collar and families live there because they can't afford to come further east, but New Haven is beneath them. It's the necessary transition zone between the have's and the have nots. It's when you start to smell something God awful is when you know you're leaving Staven and heading into New Haven. And that's the smell we all desire. You see, we come to New Haven for one reason: alcohol. We know we're too young for fake id's and since we now have a couple of upperclassmen friends who drive, for five bucks a head they'll take us to the city and we can buy booze. True, the liquor stores won't give us the time of day, but the bums and junkies hanging outside the door happily fill our trunks with beer, vodka, rum, and whiskey for a sixer of Bud or a pint of Jack. And twenty five minutes later the cold waters of the local streams and rivers serve as the refrigerators for the night.

So it was in the woods where most of my friends were tonight, though I guess it was really early morning on Sunday, but I'm still going to call it Saturday since it all started on Saturday, that life changed. While I sat home reading *This Boy's Life*, my mom peaked into my room ever so slowly with tears in her eyes.

Harris had died.

I looked at the clock and it was approaching two in the morning. I hadn't even heard the phone ringing–I still wasn't allowed to have one in my room even though I was unofficially ungrounded–because I was totally involved in Blackwell's book. But none of that mattered. Harris was dead. And I didn't know why. Mom did.

3/24/02

He had to be home before Saturday became Sunday. So he left. He never made it home.

That's what Haley tells me as the sun is rising.

3/24/02

Words can never replace emotions and feelings. They cannot take an action back nor can they solve a tangible problem. I can't find the words to express the loss and sorrow that I feel in my heart. Yet, I know that I must be the selfish one. I haven't lost my own life, I haven't lost a child, a brother, or a family member. Though I've lost my best friend, I know it can't be the same loss Harris' parents feel. But I blame them.

Harris' parents required him to be home by midnight. Ever since the New Year's Eve party when they found out he'd been drinking. They just assumed they could eliminate the partying by making him come home. But I think they made things even worse. He had to be home, otherwise curfew would be earlier. Harris had only had his driver's license for four months or so, he was one of the first of our clan to have his license. His parents never let him leave town, so technically he didn't break that rule by being at the river.

Part of me wishes that Blackwell never gave me the book to read. I probably would've succumbed to my loneliness and joined the river gang. If I were there, I would've kept Harris from driving. I know I would've. Some drunk asshole killed my grandfather a couple years back and I swore I'd never let anybody else I knew die that way.

I failed.

Mom always told me to never get into the car with somebody who'd been drinking and that I could always call her if I felt like I was in trouble.

I think Harris' parents took another approach. In my heart, I assume they wanted nothing but the best for their son. They wanted to protect him. They wanted to make sure he came home at night and slept safely in their home.

But Harris planted his car into a tree tonight.

A small part of me feels some kind of relief that he didn't kill somebody else; that he was alone. The drunk that killed my grandfather walked away from the crash. My grandfather died there.

Harris had to be home. He knew that. But he didn't have to drive. Haley tells me he was really fucked up and that everybody tried to stop him. But nobody actually stopped him. I would've stopped him.

I refuse to leave my room today. I only talk to Haley on the phone. I think about calling Jennifer to tell her what happened. But she never liked my friends in the first place, so I don't.

Throughout the day Mom comes in to check on me. I can tell she's put on her sweetest voice to try and soothe me, but I can also tell that there are many questions she wants to ask me. I don't blame her. Perhaps she's starting to discover the lies that are my life.

I can see the sun beginning to cast its long shadow on the day and I feel like exploding. I throw on my running shoes and start running toward the beech for no particular reason. It just makes me feel better for a moment.

3/24/02

The night won't allow me to sleep. I feel my heart racing as I try to calm myself down. But numbers on the alarm clock keep changing one by one and sleep will not become of me. I don't really have an image of Harris dying in my mind. It's just an overwhelming sadness.

It's not the sadness that I'm accustomed to feeling. I remember those days all too clearly. The not wanting to get out of bed and the crying encompassing my soul like a suffocating pillow over my face. It's not that type of sadness. I don't hurt for myself, but for others. I dread going to school tomorrow and having to see so many of my friends mourning and crying. I tell myself that I won't be one of them. I promise I'll be the rock, but I don't know why.

For an instant, I wanted to blame God and yell at him for taking my best friend. All those phony justifications about it being His plan when it was really Harris getting too drunk and crashing his car. It's pretty simple really. But I know he didn't have to die, and that's what's keeping me up right now. I'm pissed at my other friends for letting him drive, and I know that they're probably pissed at themselves too. Time is a healer, but it cannot be reversed.

3/25/02

Principal Matthews made the announcement approximately two minutes after the late bell rang that Harris had died. She called for a moment of silence and thought (we're not allowed to pray at public school). She then read all of the viewing and funeral information.

Nobody was shocked. News coverage had been extensive over the last 24 hours.

We were encouraged to see grief counselors. I never quite understood their purpose. I have no desire to tell a stranger all of my feelings about somebody dying...who she didn't know either.

Classes continued as scheduled and teachers all seemed tense and hurried to get to their lessons and avoid all mention of Harris. Staring at his empty seat in Blackwell's class is when it finally hits me though. Harris and I only have one shared class, and not having to look at his empty seat until now helped to ease the pain. But now that feeling is rushing back to me. Mr. Blackwell senses it and covertly asks me if I'm alright. Though I tell him yes, he knows the answer is no. He asks me to stay after class and I willingly oblige.

I don't really know what to tell Blackwell, but I don't think it really matters. Having seen my sickly depressed stage a week back, Blackwell seems to be making sure I'm not suicidal.

I'm not.

The sorrow for Harris is so much different than the sorrow for myself. As I think about it, the self sorrow I loathe myself for from time to time is genuinely pathetic. I have nothing to be depressed about. And yet, when I shouldn't be I am, and now I'm not, even though such a feeling could be justified.

So Blackwell and I softly talk about Harris and the decisions that people make and the lessons to be learned. Though I know much of this already, it feels good just to know that Blackwell cares. Mom's been great and she's been very kind to me; I think I'll tell my dad tonight, but he'll probably just ask me which one was Harris.

3/27/02

I don't go to funerals. Mostly because I hate finality and knowing that there is no other way; but also it's the silence of something I don't believe in. During the wake, I watched Harris' family say the rosary and turn to their priest for comfort and guidance. Hundreds of well-wishers offered prayers and blessings. Harris' mother and father talked proudly of their son and the many great things God had in store for him. But I don't believe any of it.

Harris crashed his car because he was drunk.

He killed himself. God didn't kill Harris. Harris killed Harris.

My best friend is dead and I weep for him. But I wonder why so many look to God's master plan as solace while ignoring the obvious: Harris should still be alive. Blame is tough to assign to those who have passed on, but ignorance is not an acceptable substitute either.

So when Jennifer tapped me on the shoulder at lunch today, I explained to her why I didn't go to Harris' funeral. I guess she felt sorry for me. The table was empty, save for my lonely self. The rest of the gang was still at church. Ever since we'd called it quits, Jennifer and I sat at separate lunch tables, but not today. We talked about a lot of things that had nothing to do with us or Harris. But small talk about track and classes can only last so long. Inevitably, she'd bring it up.

"You seem to be handling this very well, Andrew," she said.

"Thanks," was all I could muster for a reply. She must have expected to see me in a million little pieces, torn and broken, brooding in my own self pity. But I wasn't. "I guess I have no real choice. Nothing is going to change what happened so I must accept that and move on."

"Oh, you know it's alright to feel bad about this."

"If you want to see me depressed, just let me know," I snapped.

"Fuck you. That's not what I meant. When we were dating you always seemed so sad. Now your best friend has died and you just brush it off."

"I'm not brushing it off. It sucks. He did something stupid, real stupid. But he did it to himself. I can't explain it." And it's the 'it' that I truly can't explain. I want to tell Jennifer that the sad Andrew she dealt with during our dating experiences was an entirely different type of feeling than the one I felt now, but I couldn't find the words. So I left her sitting all by herself.

Jennifer's words about me being so depressed all of the time when we dated irritated me for the rest of the day.

The happiest days of my life were when I dated her. True, there were a couple of days where I was depressed, she dumped me on one of them, but I seem to remember a lot of great days too. But perception and reality are isolated to the person living in the moment. Perhaps my state of happiness was still depressing to her. I don't want to live my life as the sad kid in the corner.

3/28/02

I've decided that I am the only person who can control my life and how I feel. I've decided that if I don't like something, then I will change it. I've decided that if I don't like how I feel, then I will do something about it.

Standing

3/30/02

As I paced near the start line readying myself for the first outdoor track meet of the year, I heard Dad screaming at me. Shocked at his presence, I saw him, Devin, and Lois waving frantically from across the track. They were bundled for a blizzard while I stood clad in my short shorts and tank top. It was about 40 degrees, a balmy late March day in central Connecticut. I don't know how they even knew the meet was here; I hadn't told them, but that didn't matter. I'm not sure if any of them had ever seen me run in a track race or in a cross country meet.

As the gun went off starting the two mile race, I found my thoughts drifting to my family being there, pretty cool. By the end of the first lap, I was running right with the leaders and felt physically strong.

Then it hit me. I was running with the leaders.

Though I'd had a decent indoor season, I was always a step behind the leaders, one of the second tier runners.

Shit.

What do I do? I couldn't believe it, I was actually looking for Bennett so I could hear him scream something at me. And he screamed, but this time I wanted to listen. "Stay relaxed up top Andrew and keep your stride open!" His words registered quickly. I opened my previously clenched fists and felt my arms and chest unwind, almost a second wind already.

That carried me for a couple of laps. *Form, stay relaxed, stride, breathing pattern, look ahead.* Those words ran loops inside of my head, but as the Windham runner drifted back, it left only me and the Bethel Public runner up front. With just 500 meters to go, I was wondering how this was all going to play out.

"NOW. GO NOW ANDREW!" My thoughts were splintered by Bennett's screams. I just did it, probably out of fear. But I did it. Instead of picking it up at the 400 meter mark and sprinting the last 200 meters, I started early. With 500 meters to go, I made my move (with Bennett's obvious insistence) and pulled away from the Bethel Public runner. By the 300 mark I didn't know where he was, but the whooping of the crowd told me he was very close.

Bennett, who usually watches from the finish line, was prancing up and down at the 200 meter mark screaming, "Go Andrew! Now, you've got to go harder...GO!"

So I did, full sprint, legs aching, lungs burning, stomach churning, mind racing and an illusive finish line in sight. As the finish line seemingly crept closer, fear placed its grip on me and I could feel my whole body tensing up. The fear of being passed. But somewhere inside of me, about 50 meters from the finish, I somehow remembered to open up my hands, and I could feel myself relax just enough to move just a little quicker. I crossed the finish line and wanted to collapse, but the thrill (or shock) of victory kept me standing. I glanced back and saw the Bethel Public runner about 5 meters back. I had clearly out kicked him.

Being high fived all around by my teammates was pretty cool. But it paled in comparison from Devin's high five and my dad's hug. Lois didn't know what to do...hug me, slap me five, or simply smile sheepishly, but it didn't matter, her awkwardness clearly expressed how proud she was.

Several minutes later, Bennett approached. I braced myself for the speech of what I should've done better and how the race didn't need to be that close.

"Sit down Andrew, listen." And here it comes, but it didn't. "Remember this race. You did everything right. You went out early. You stayed up front. You listened. I told you to go at 500 meters because you're a cross country runner and have extra endurance. He could out sprint you, but not if you forced him to sprint for more than a lap. And you did that. All of that work you did during the break paid off today. Great job. I'm proud of you, kid."

"Thanks, coach."

"Remember this race, Andrew. When you don't feel like doing your homework, remember this race and how good it felt to win. You can't run without the grades. When you want to cut corners at practice, remember this race. When you're cursing me at practice and can't figure out why I'm on you, remember this race."

His diabolical smile at the end of his speech revealed too much. Bennett knew how I felt about him, but it didn't matter at this moment.

Winning felt great. Bennett's approval felt even better. I thought having my dad, step mom, and Devin watching was the best, but when my mom tapped me on the shoulder to congratulate me, that was the best. I didn't even know she'd come. Quietly, she slipped in and sat in the stands away from everyone else. She just watched.

On the bus ride home, I knew she'd called my dad. I knew she told him I needed some support right now, because of Harris. I knew she was worried about me. I knew she really must have swallowed her pride to beg my father to come stand in the cold to watch me run in circles. You know what though, in the end, I don't think he minded and I think it was worth it to my mom.

Did I ever tell you how much I love my mom?

3/31/02

"Get up and eat while Layne showers. I left your breakfast on the table. Hurry boys, we don't want to be late for Easter mass. I don't want all them damn heathens to get all of the seats" And that's how Sunday always begins.

Next to a bagel, yogurt, and juice, was a newspaper clipping. It was the results of yesterday's race. Mom had highlighted my first place finish. Believe it or not, it was the first time I'd seen the time. I was so caught up in winning, I never even bothered to check my time. The paper said I ran 10 minutes and 22 seconds. By far my best, but I knew I had to break 10 minutes to have a shot at making the state championship race and be below 9:45 to have any chance at competing for a medal. Mom also left a napkin with a note on it saying 'great job!'

It's funny, seeing my time left me feeling almost, disappointed. I was in limbo. I was happy I'd won, but now I wanted to keep winning. And if I wanted to be a state champion, this time was flat out unacceptable. There was work to be done. And I welcomed the challenge.

4/1/02

I apologized to Jennifer today, you know, for that whole unpleasant incident in the cafeteria last week when I left her all alone at the table after snapping at her. She said she understood and that I was under a lot of pressure.

She also congratulated me on my race. I guess we're talking again.

At lunch I realized I have no real friends. I sat at the same table and listened to them rehash what they did over the weekend. It primarily involved getting very wasted. The acceptable reason was to blow off steam from what happened with Harris dying. I just sat there thinking about how it was the very same thing that essentially killed Harris. And I know that I've been guilty too. But it just didn't seem appropriate right then.

Telling the guys about my weekend must have seemed pretty pathetic. On Friday I went to bed early to prepare for the track meet. On Saturday I went out to dinner with my mom then read the rest of *This Boy's Life*. I'm such a happening teenager.

I was anxious to see how Bennett would treat me today at practice. Part of me was hoping for the same old, same old where Bennett would clearly pick on my every move while overlooking the idiocy of some of the other runners' moves. And yet there was a definite part of me hoping that I would somehow find myself in Bennett's good graces and I'd be the golden child. I decided before practice today that I wanted to be a state champion so I had to start working like one. I separated myself from the normal knuckleheads I hang with and stretched by myself. While Bennett spoke, I looked him straight in the eye and avoided making my normal smirks, sighs, and comments. As we prepared for our distance run, with Bennett trailing in his car, I tried to focus solely on the task, consistent mile times with loose form. Around mile three, Bennett barked that I was too tight and to loosen up. He yelled that again at mile four and five. By mile seven I had rectified that problem, but I'm not sure how much Bennett could see as he parked his car and we reentered the track.

As practiced ended, Bennett yelled good job, your miles were quick and consistent. I couldn't believe it, did he end with a compliment and not remind me of being too tight?

I guess that's our compromise, he yells at me throughout practice while people can hear, but he pats me on the back in private. I can live with that.

4/5/02

I actually have something to do tonight besides sitting at home and reading. A lot of things had to come together for this to happen. Even though Mom had slackened considerably on the whole being grounded thing, today I was officially released. Except for a B in math, I had straight A's. I don't think I could believe it. Very few teachers put comments, except Blackwell who put 'exceeds course objectives.' I find it odd how pretty much every teacher had the time to comment when I was falling short, but now that I'm 'meeting my potential,' the comments have disappeared. Oh well.

During the week I decided I didn't want to hang out with the same old people–the ones I used to party with all weekend. I wanted different friends who actually did stuff, the problem, though, was that I therefore had no friends. And that's when Jennifer reappeared.

On Wednesday I was sitting by myself at lunch, you know, hanging with my new peer group, me, when she plopped down right next to me. With an emphatic "So," she asked me why I was sitting alone, and I explained the whole situation to her.

"But you don't have any other friends Andrew," was her immediate reply.

"That's why I'm sitting alone."

"You know, you're really strange. I don't get you. I mean I think it's cool that you want to do stuff besides just drinking on weekends, but you don't have to give up on all of your friends in the process."

"Yes, Jennifer, I do. We have nothing in common anymore. They just want to party and I don't. I'd rather go to a play or a concert or anything. Every time I see a beer bottle I think about Harris, and I know that they've learned nothing, but I've learned something. I'm not sure exactly what, but I want to experience everything that life has to offer me."

"So what are you doing this weekend."

"I have no friends, so I'll probably just read at home or hang out with my mom."

"Now that's experiencing everything that life has to offer, Andrew."

And that's when she said it. She just blurted it out–why not the two of us just find something to do. Anything, something different, something cool. After practice we both searched the internet and newspaper for cool things to do, I stumbled upon a special evening exhibition at the New Haven Rail and Trolley Museum. Evening rides on historic trains from the New Haven Line and one dollar admission to the museum.

This is probably a good time to tell you that I'm obsessed with trains. When I was younger, I used to pretend I was a conductor and make station announcements while riding in the car with my parents. Every time we crossed a town line I'd make an announcement. When I was really bored I'd make schedules complete with destinations, amenities, and fares. A few years ago I got to go on a ride along in a commuter train. Mom had somehow arranged that with the train crew and surprised me one day. I even got to blow the horn and everything.

Jennifer had never been to the museum before; she worried about getting there, but I told her we could just take the commuter train into New Haven and walk to the museum. I'd done it several times before, but apparently her parents needed some convincing. They finally came around, though.

Even though I'd been to the museum several times before and ridden on the trolleys numerous times, going with Jennifer was an entirely new experience. One of the museum exhibits had features on the New Haven line stations, including the historic depot in our town. The station had laid dormant for decades, but recently a new station was built to accommodate commuter rail; Jennifer never knew the history of the station. But the best part of the night was dinner. The museum has several dining cars reliving the glory days of rail travel. We dined in an old parlour car from the historic California Zephyr. Complete with real dinnerware and a wait staff wearing historic uniforms, the meal was quite impressive, both with flavor and price. But since the entrance fee was only a dollar, I didn't mind springing for dinner.

Because the experience was so new to Jennifer and one that I knew by heart, most of dinner involved her asking me questions about everything from the dining car we were in to the last trolley we rode. For once my obsession with trains made me cool and not some pathetic loser. In middle school my older brother used to purposefully derail my electric trains, then laugh. I'd spend hours setting up villages and crossings, bridges and tunnels, then, when I wasn't around, Mark would run the trains at full speed around sharp turns, derailing every car and annihilating my towns. Watching me cry, yell, and scream, he'd just call me names and laugh in my face. I told Jennifer about my train collection–three working electric sets as well as several model cars, engines, and historic spikes and ties–afraid she'd just laugh in my face too. But she didn't. She asked if she could see them one day.

4/10/02

I knew she'd bring it up at some point. How could she not? After all, according to her it was the reason we'd broken up.

This week Jennifer sat with me at lunch everyday. Not because she had to, I hope, but because she wanted to. It was just the two of us. Conversation was pretty easy. At first we talked about the train museum and then track–she too noticed that Bennett didn't hate me nearly as much as he used to. But by Wednesday, our conversation stalled.

"So do you still get that depressed feeling?" I couldn't blame her for asking. I knew she didn't like hanging out with me when I felt that way. I mean I can't blame her; it's not like a depressed kid is the barrel of laughs a teenage girl is seeking out.

"It's different. When Harris died I expected to feel sad all of the time. But I didn't. I was upset that he died and it hurt, but I had to accept it, plus I knew his death could've been prevented. I told Blackwell that, and he seemed to understand. And it's like in these books he's having me read, everybody has shit to deal with. I've got to deal with my own shit and move on. There's no point in feeling sorry for myself."

"But what do you do when you feel that way?"

"I don't know, I just focus on what I enjoy and set goals for myself. That feeling really hasn't been coming around much anymore anyways. I know there's things I want to do with my life and I'm going to do them."

I was glad Jennifer and I had that conversation. Hearing myself say those words and believing them was reassuring. There are so many things that I want to do with my life and I am the only one who can make sure that it happens.

4/12/02

Blackwell and I finally discussed *This Boy's Life* today. With all that had happened in the past month, it felt like an eternity since I started reading it. Today's discussion was much different than so many of the others we had. I think it was mostly my doing because I actually understood the message for once.

"It is about finding your identity," Blackwell confirmed my assertion. "Much like Tobias tries to rid himself of his step father, run away, and change his name, I want you too to find your identity."

"You remember, how you told me that I follow and don't lead, well I thought a lot about that in this book. Tobias does his own thing, but he's running from who he really is and creating a person that he's not. I don't think I'd ever run away or forge an application, but I know I have to decide who I want to be."

"And who is it that you want to be?" questioned Mr. Blackwell.

"Don't laugh. I want to be me. I know that sounds stupid, but I don't want to make decisions because I think it will make me cool or because it's what people expect of me. I want to see the world; so I'm going to. I want to win the state championship in cross country and track, and I'm going to work my ass off until I do. I want to see the Pacific Ocean and climb the Red Rocks in Sedona. I want to take a train across the country and I want to play guitar while sitting on the city dock of Annapolis. I want to live every moment of my life."

"How."

"What do you mean?"

"Andrew, those are all great things and I hope you do all of them, but how will you make it all happen?"

"I don't know. I know I have to get a job to pay for it. I'll probably go to college. I was thinking about it, I could do some of it in college, you know like study abroad and work in the summers."

"You think you'll go to college?"

"Yeah."

"Andrew, college is where you're going if I have to drag you there myself; you're not wasting your potential."

"Exactly Mr. Blackwell, if my potential is realized by going to college and that's where I want to go, then I'll do it, but I'm not doing it because I feel like I have to."

"Without an education you have nothing to fall back on."

"True, and when I fall I'm the only one who can be blamed and I'm the only one who can pick me up."

"Andrew, I'm afraid you're missing the point all together."

"No, you opened my eyes and now I'm beginning to see. I know I'll need help along the way and people will give me advice, but only I can take charge of my life and only I can decide where I go with it. I promise I won't waste it, but I'm going to live it."

"Read this." And with that Blackwell tossed me *On the Road* by Jack Kerouac and wished me luck in tomorrow's race.

4/13/02

I ran a good time in the two mile today, but Jenkevich of New London beat me handily. Bennett said I ran a decent race. I have a lot of work to do if I want to compete with the best.

Since I have no friends, except Jennifer I guess, I had nothing to do tonight, so I started reading *On the Road*, it's not quite what I expected. I'd never heard of this Kerouac fellow and I wasn't expecting a travel diary, but this book is...I don't know. Have you read it? I'm a little lost, so far the main character Sal Paradise (that last name must mean something, but I haven't figured it out yet) is hitchhiking across America trying to find his buddies...I guess I better keep going.

4/14/02

Typically, Sundays are supposed to be off days for runners; but I've decided that I need extra running if I'm going to make it to States. Though I've been warned about burning out, I also know that the season only has six weeks left and I can recover over the summer. Additionally, the day before a meet is always an easy day–a mile, sometimes less, and stretching. So I figure if I take Sundays off I'm really taking two off days.

Long distance runs are the best way to recover after a race. Knowing we had to go to mass, I roused myself before seven and crept quietly downstairs to stretch. Leaving my house, I had no preset route, but I always enjoy running by the beach. Though by no means warm, Spring was clearly starting to win its annual battle with Winter; the air was crisp, moist, refreshing.

Only a mile from my house, I can usually start to smell the beach from a half mile away. I love everything about the beach. And as I made my Sunday morning approach, my whole body felt a sense of belonging like I've never quite experienced before. Though I planned to run on the street that runs parallel to the beach for about 2 miles, I decided to ditch that plan, along with my shoes. Barefoot, I ran along the sand absorbing the sights of seagulls and shells with the sounds of the lapping waves and flowing breezes. Occasionally a stray passerby would wave a hand in greeting.

A rocky shore intercepts the sand at the point where the parallel road cuts away from the beach, and with that, I u-turned and headed back to my shoes, two miles away. This time I chose to run in the water, freeing my toes of the sand that had encrusted them. Though the water still held much of winter's chill, my feet responded fleetly and carried me two miles back to my point of origin.

Now five miles into my run, I initially planned to lace up my shoes and continue the last mile home. Bad idea. My feet were soaked and very red. I didn't want to stop and lose my heart rate, so I simply grabbed my shoes and headed for home. Fearing blisters, cuts, and scrapes, I ran mostly on the locals' lawns for the last mile. Partially abused, my feet greatly welcomed the sight of my house.

4/15/02

Lunch is a tricky proposition these days. Just a few weeks ago it was simple. It was sort of like we had assigned seats. Not only did we always sit at the same table, but we also all sat in the same seats. Harris died. I moved away. But the rest of the gang–Darrin, Chris, Mike, Adam, and Bobby–they all sit just the same. The day after I left, a couple girls joined them; I think they're freshmen, at least that's what Jennifer said. So usually lunch starts off with me sitting by myself. Then periodically one of the guys will walk by and cough 'faggot' behind me or 'loser' in my ear. Occasionally they toss bits of food at me. I think it's safe to say that they no longer like me. But I don't quite understand why. I chose to sit at another table one day, in fact, they never really even asked me about it. The day I moved Darrin asked me why I was sitting at a different table, and I simply said because I felt like it. None of them even tried to come and sit with me. And none of them asked me to come back and sit with them. But what I don't understand is why they pick on me now. At least I'm discovering who my friends really are, in multiple ways.

And then there's the whole Jennifer situation. Everyday with about five minutes left in lunch, after I'm done eating and while I'm perusing a book (currently *On the Road* still), Jennifer plops down next to me. Perhaps 'plops' carries too much of a negative connotation. I do welcome her presence. So I guess Jennifer *sits* down next to me. I don't know if she comes over because she truly wants to, or if she feels sorry for me. Today she asked me what I did over the weekend and the only thing I could really tell her about was my run on Sunday. Kind of pathetic, I thought to myself. But she didn't see it that way. She thought I was partially crazy, but admired my connection to the shore and the whole barefoot part. That's what I love about Jennifer, she finds my eccentricities refreshing and cool, not weird and dorky.

Shit. I said it. That word. LOVE.

Lately I've been thinking about it a lot. I don't think I ever stopped loving Jennifer, but with Harris' death and finding myself, I had pretty much put my feelings for Jennifer on hold. That is, until we went to the train museum and had dinner, that was it. She had my heart again. Plus, she sits with me at lunch and seems genuinely interested in me again, but I fear it's just pity. I want to tell her this, but I don't want to drive her away, especially if she really is my friend, my only friend.

Back to lunch, so finally Jennifer asked me if I wanted to sit at her table for lunch. Sure, she said, it would be just a bunch of freshmen girls, but that at least I wouldn't have to sit alone. Though I'm pretty sure she was genuine in her offer, I quickly declined citing how I didn't mind being by myself. But I told Jennifer she could sit with me anytime she wanted. For one minute, for the whole lunch, or for no time at all. I didn't want her to feel sorry for me. True, I wanted her to plop (sit) down next to me everyday, but only if she wanted to. My theory was this, if she chose to join me, then there was a good chance we'd get back together. But if she chose to leave me be, then I'd know she only visited for pity, and it was time to forget her.

But her answer only muddied the waters more. She simply said "Ok."

And that's when I made my move. No, I didn't kiss her, though in retrospect, perhaps that would've been the better course of action.

No, instead, I said, "Jennifer, when you see me, do you still see only the depressed sickly Andrew that you hated so much."

"Why are you asking me this?"

"Because I've been trying so hard to leave that person behind. That's why I changed my friends–they were part of my demise and I knew it. It's also why I run on the beach, because I like it and it makes me feel good. I'm trying to be the person that I've always envisioned myself as being. And that person is happy, unique, and living life to the fullest–not wallowing in my own misery. Jennifer, I feel so much better."

"Andrew, we need to talk."

And that's when the dismissal bell rang.

4/15/02

For the rest of the day, all I could think about was how Jennifer wanted to talk. Blackwell's class was a blur, though I did learn that Giles Corey (from *The Crucible*) was pressed to death; what a terrible way to go.

And practice was no better. I couldn't focus. And Bennett must have been licking his chops at noticing my off-beat performance. During practice he gave me a good yell several times about my form and paying attention to what I was doing. Typically, I would curse Bennett for being so harsh on me. Except, this time I knew he was right. What I was dreading would be the post-practice tirade. Recently he'd been patting me on the back after practice and even encouraging me with positive words. But when he told me to stay after, I knew I was a goner and my few weeks of paradise had met its stormy end.

But I wasn't a goner at all.

"What's bothering you today?" Bennett asked.

Shocked at the concern in his voice, I simply replied, "I don't know. I just don't feel right today; I can't focus. I feel fine physically."

"Shake it off kid, we all have those days. Just try to focus on your goals. Remember, you said you want to go to States. Every kid in this state is going to have a bad day, be glad yours occurred at practice and not during a race. Come back strong tomorrow," Bennett concluded.

"I will coach. Sorry about today."

And with that our conversation was over.

Bennett made a lot of sense. I did want to go to States and I certainly needed to practice better than today. I know I allowed my impending conversation with Jennifer to weigh me down. And that's the very type of thing I promised myself that I wouldn't allow to happen. If I wanted to accomplish something, then I must put forth the effort to do it. Bennett was right, everybody has a bad day, and thankfully, I had mine today and not in a qualifying race.

Walking out of the locker room, Jennifer caught me mid-stride. Obviously, she had been waiting for me and was ready to talk.

And she started right away, "Andrew, let's talk now so we can do it in person."

"Ok," was all I could muster for a reply.

Jennifer continued immediately, with a pace that told me she'd been rehearsing this many times over in her head, "Andrew, you need to know this is hard for me because I've never felt this way about anyone before. In some ways I love you so much, especially when we're hanging out having fun, like at the museum or when we went to the Village for dinner. But I also remember the days where you just seemed to be so upset about everything. I couldn't stand those days. And now when I look at you I don't know who I see. You seem happy, yet sit by yourself in lunch. You have all of these plans and aspirations, but you do them all alone. Part of me wants to be with you, but part of me fears being with you. I don't want to get hurt all over again, but I don't want to lose you either."

I believed everything she said. Mostly because in my own mind that's exactly how I expected her to see things. I think I shocked her with my reply, "Jennifer, how about we just be friends for a while. I'll tell you what I'm doing and if you want to do it too, then we'll do it together. If not, no hard feelings. And if you want to do something with me, just ask and I'll respond the same way. No pressure. Same thing with lunch. If you want to sit with me when I'm alone, do so, but only because you want to. And if I want to sit at your table, I will, but only because I want to."

Jennifer just smiled at me, like a burden even too large for Atlas had been removed from her shoulders. She kissed me on the cheek, and said, "Thanks."

And with that, our conversation was over.

4/16/02

I ate lunch by myself today for the whole period. I was fine with that. I had a great practice.

4/17/02

Jennifer ate the whole lunch with me today. I was fine with that. I had a great practice.

4/19/02

The track meet in Middletown was my best race last year. I'm looking forward to it today because I've had good practices since Monday's debacle, I ran well here last year, plus I get another crack at Jenkevich of New London, though he's probably not the favorite as Weaver of Killingly is expected to run today. On the bus Bennett called me to his seat. He wanted to discuss my times.

"Realistically, Andrew, we have to shave seconds, not fractions of seconds off of your lap times."

I liked how Bennett used 'we.' Sure, it was me running, but by using 'we' it signaled to me that he believed in my ability to make States and that he was going to do everything he could to help me. It used to be 'you.' As in 'you' didn't run enough, 'you' didn't listen, 'you' need to do more. But now it was 'we.'

The two mile is really a simple race. Unlike the 800 where one bad move can ruin your whole race, the two mile (3200 meters) allows room for error. Eight laps. That's it. Quite simply put the first and last lap are usually fast, but the race is won and lost in the middle.

"To qualify for States, Andrew," Bennet continued, "we need to get you down to 10 flat. You've got the time to do it, but we have to look at whole seconds per lap and not half seconds per lap. I recorded your lap times during your last two races, your ran a 10:19 and a 10:18. Once you're in shape, and you are, it's hard to lower your time. Little things will pay off, good sleep, healthy diet, focused practices, and clearly defined goals. I want you to run 10:12 today. Here's why, in your last two races your first lap was 69 seconds and your last was 71. Your middle laps were in the upper 70's to low 80's. For a 10 flat you need to average 75 seconds over eight laps. You can do that. Rather than overloading you with information, as you begin each lap I'll tell you what to run. If you're too fast, I'll give you a slower lap, if you're too slow I'll give you a faster lap. You know your first lap is 69. Run a 69 to start, then I'll yell a 73 at you. Got it. Run a 70 and I'll yell a 72 to make up for the missing second. Ok."

"Alright. I can do that. Am I really losing ten seconds during the middle?"

"Yes and no, everybody loses time in the middle. The body recovers from the adrenaline of the start and tires, until the last lap where it gives all it has. My goal is to keep your body from tiring as much in the middle. Your goal is to keep your adrenaline up for more than just first and last lap."

"Ok, thanks coach."

I like how Bennett gave each of us a goal. By giving me times, he figured he was helping to train me. Similarly, by making each lap a race against the clock, I knew my adrenaline would kick it up a notch. Interestingly, Bennett focused none of his pre-race discussion on winning the race or the other runners. Perhaps he was focusing beyond the race at hand and looking at the long term goal; I know I was.

The race was a blur. All I remember were numbers. I don't even remember the other runners being out there. Bennett screamed 75 for lap two and I was shocked that I had opened with a 67, but with Weaver and Jenkevich in front of me, I felt like the poor child in tow. As soon as Bennett yelled 75, I knew my race was over, but I was committed to running his time. It was we, not I.

I finished second. Weaver won, but Jenkevich must've burnt himself out trying to keep up with Weaver. Weaver ran a 9:57. Jenkevich ran a 10:14. I ran a 10:12. Right on the money.

On the bus ride home, I decided to sit with Bennett.

"I was kind of all over the place coach. Some laps I was too fast so you had to slow me down. Then, I was too slow and you had to speed me up."

"Just what I was expecting Andrew. We've done very little work with pacing. You're still learning what a 70 second lap feels like as compared to a 75 or 80 second lap. We'll work on it in practice. But you hit your goal today. And that's all that matters. Hey, how the hell did you beat Jenkevich, I didn't see that coming."

I laughed, "Me neither, I thought I had no shot after you screamed 75 for lap two. He must've burnt himself out."

"Exactly!" Bennett's enthusiasm surprised me, "see Andrew, he ran Weaver's race, not his own. You ran your race today and beat him. Keep running your race and things will be just fine."

After Bennett and I finished our chat, I turned to grab a seat on the bus. Usually I'm one of the first ones on and sit by myself, but since I went directly to Bennett upon boarding, there were no empty seats when our conversation concluded. And it dawned on me, I have no friends on the team. Well, there is of course Jennifer, but she always sits with Amy. I really didn't know what to do, being alone was cool, and I remember having friends, but now, I couldn't be alone and I had no friends. So I went and sat with Jake, a freshman distance runner who was sitting alone. I figured since he was a freshman (and not very good) that he wouldn't mind having me, a sophomore–and the current star, sitting with him. Remember when Shepherd was the star, but he's still 'nursing' his injuries and barely able to run competitively. Jake said nothing the whole ride home. Neither did I. Perfect.

Tonight, Sal Paradise reunited with Dean Moriarity, who I met for the first time. Dean epitomized everything I wanted to be in life, free. True, Dean failed at times, but he never allowed failure to or fear of failure to impede upon his next journey.

4/22/02

School started off with a moment of silence for the victims of Columbine High School; though the tragedy occurred on April 20th, since that was a Saturday our school reflected today. I remember exactly where I was when the terror struck. Sitting in seventh grade language arts class, Mrs. Rendezvick knocked on my teacher's door. It was towards the end of the school day, Mrs. Erikson returned from the door, frozen. For a moment, I could tell that she was contemplating something very deeply. Later, I realized that she was calculating whether she should deliver the news immediately, or at the end of the period. She chose immediately.

I don't remember her exact words, I remember her voice trembling and the tears falling down her face. For the first time all year, our class was silent.

Outside, the sun shone brightly, all I could think about was how beautiful of a day it was, and what if one of my classmates did the same thing.

During the moment of silence, I thought about what life must've been like for the students at Columbine as they observed this anniversary. In my own little world, my life was so important, and all of the little things that were *so important* were the center of my universe. But none of it was important.

It's a cliche, I know, but I thought about how I must live every day like it was the last day, and that I may not have another tomorrow so I better make today count. It's a cliche, I know it, but I'm sure the students of Columbine felt who was dating who for prom was so important, until, well it happened. And those little things were just that: little. I am no prophet and I'm barely able to form a coherent sentence at times, but I am learning to value what matters, I hope.

April 23, 2002

Perhaps one true oddity in this world is that my parents were born on the same day in the same year. They're turning 43 tomorrow. Every year we alternate which parent we spend the day with. This year it's with Mom, so that means Layne and I will call Dad after school and go out to dinner with Mom and exchange gifts–I still haven't picked one out yet. When we were much younger, dinner meant Burger King, compliments of Mom's three children. I guess that was a night off from cooking for Mom, but probably not the birthday dinner she imagined. Similarly, in those days a gift generally meant a chocolate bar and a cheap bottle of perfume. This year, I want to get her something special, I just have no clue as to what.

Dad's birthdays were always different. If we had school, our step-mom would pick us up and we'd drive up to Dad's office to greet him. Then, we'd go out to a fancy dinner that Lois would pay for, exchange gifts, then be driven back to Mom's. Dad's gifts were no better than Mom's. Usually a CD or a baseball t-shirt.

Over the last few years, our gifts have gotten substantially better. Mom usually ends up with a nice piece of jewelry that Mark picked out and Dad some kind of newfangled electronic contraption, also picked out by Mark. With Mark being at college, this year the burden falls upon me.

At school today I explained the quandary to Mr. Blackwell. I told him that I wanted to get Mom something special, I had no clue what to get her, and that I had no money.

"What about your father?" Mr. Blackwell questioned.

"I haven't thought about that either," I responded.

And that was problematic too. I wanted to get my father something nice too, but it wasn't as important to me. I knew it was because I lived with Mom and felt more of a connection to her, I just hope that didn't make me a bad person.

"A job, that's what you need," Mr. Blackwell chuckled.

His idea made sense. I could use some spending money. I was turning 16 in a few weeks and wanted a car, which I knew I'd have to pay for. But his suggestion made no sense for the moment. How could I get a job, work, and be paid in time for my parents' birthdays–which were tomorrow!

"How much money do you have Andrew."

"Probably $200 leftover from shoveling snow all winter."

"Get a job. But before you do that, simply buy your mom some flowers, a nice card, and a nice meal. Take her to Sound Side or the Steven's Inn. Then, this weekend when you see your dad, take him to a ball game for some father-son time."

It was true, dinner would probably cost $80 bucks or so and Layne might throw in a twenty. Plus, my dad loves going to minor league baseball games, he never has anyone to go with him, and that should only run another 30 or 40 bucks. That was the plan.

I had a separate practice from everybody else. Bennett said that since I was running on Sundays that my regular workout schedule needed to be adjusted. He couldn't 'tell' me to run on Sundays because that was against state rules, but he was ecstatic that I discovered the benefits for myself. So while most of the team did a middle distance run, Bennett had me running 400 meter sprints, 68 seconds apiece, 68 second break between each one. If I was over 68, I lost it from my break time. If I was under 68, that became my break time. I ran 10 intervals; my worst was 71, that meant a 65 second break; my best was 66, that meant a 66 second break.

After the workout, Bennett explained the duality of the workout. One: allow my body to feel what a 68 felt like and to be able to notice differences of being too fast or too slow. Second: to allow my body to run tired. Bennett said he knew that I couldn't run 8 consecutive 68 second laps during a race, but I needed to open with a 68 and not fall off so dramatically during the middle of the race. Workouts like this would help build my leg and lung strength so my 'slow' laps wouldn't be so slow.

I asked Bennett about the other runners, wouldn't they notice that I was getting special treatment. He said absolutely; and they may hate it. If they do, tell them to run with me and they'll get the same treatment. Bennett pointed out that I showed up in shape, they didn't, I was putting in extra effort, they weren't.

"Shepherd used to do that. But since he got injured, he's just thrown in the towel," Bennett remarked.

"I hated how Shepherd got special treatment," I blurted in reply.

"I know," Bennett replied without any emotion.

I think I hated Shepherd's special treatment because he was a prick about it. I vowed to be positive and supportive of my teammates, though none of them, save Jennifer, were my friends.

April 24, 2002

As soon as I awoke, I left a card containing information regarding our evening's reservations. Mom was shocked.

She hadn't received her flowers yet, mostly because we didn't have them. Since I had practice after school, Layne agreed to go into town to buy a dozen roses nicely arranged. I knew he'd hate to have to walk the twenty minutes to town and back, but I told him if he paid for the flowers, I'd take care of dinner. Plus, I'm pretty sure he knew Mom would really appreciate it and we didn't have many other options

I walked home from practice and beat Mom home by like two minutes. She was in the door before I could grab my shower or inspect Layne's purchase. Thankfully, he'd come through. I must say, the flowers were beautiful; more perfect than what I would've picked out.

Mom's reaction was priceless. She loved them. Layne even put a little card in the middle of the bouquet indicating it was from both of us. Mom said she couldn't believe it, and Mark had flowers delivered to her office and called to wish a happy birthday.

I don't think Mom had received flowers in ten years, now twice in the same day. She was elated! Home and office would both be bright, she exclaimed.

****

Though I knew we were cutting it close, I burst out of the shower and quickly called Dad at the office to wish him my best. I'd called Lois before practice to tell her of our Saturday baseball game idea, she thought it was perfect.

The only other time I'd been to Sound Side was for New Year's several years back; I think I ordered from the kids' menu. The 'adult' menu was quite impressive. Layne was going through his vegetarian stage and he found some vegan acorn dish on the menu, whatever, Mom found the seafood, and I found the steak.

Preparing for the worst, I had pretty much emptied my bank account. I prepared for the price of the food and drinks, but had forgotten about dessert. Though I told the person who answered the phone yesterday that it was my mom's birthday, I was still shocked that the waiter brought out three pieces of cake without prompting. Dessert was awesome, despite the hilarity of the wait staff signing in seven different keys with seven different ranges of emotion–apparently they've played this charade out before. The best part of dessert: it was FREE!

So when the bill came, it wasn't too bad: $68 plus I left an extra fifteen for tip. I still had 50 dollars in the bank and 64 dollars in my pocket and the burning feeling of knowing that Mom's birthday was a success!

April 27, 2002

We had practice at seven this morning. I remember how that used to bother me. But now that my Friday nights consist mostly of reading (I'll tell you about last night's reading in a little bit, but I have a lot to cover right now), I don't mind the early start to my Saturday. And today I needed it.

Home from practice by nine, I scarfed down breakfast, showered, and biked to town. Ironically, I rode to where Mom was: the grocery store. I've become so used to not having rides or just not thinking about it, I didn't even think to ask if Mom was going into town. Anyways, I figured it was definitely time for a job and I figured I'd spread my application around. Most places want you to be 16, but I figured that I'd be 16 in just about two weeks and wouldn't hurt to get a head start. The grocery store had a huge sign that said "ON SITE INTERVIEWS TODAY." Immediately I went in and saw a little table set-up for potential applicants. I was the only visitor.

As soon as I finished filling out the application, I sat down with one of the managers. She told me that I could only work 15 hours a week until I was 16, but that was no problem since my birthday was so close. I told her that I couldn't work that much yet because I had track until the end of May and that Sunday was the only day I could guarantee being free. Luckily, that worked for them since nobody ever wanted to work Sundays. She looked in her computer and told me that I could work bagging groceries and clearing the parking lots on Sundays for up to ten hours at $7.25 an hour. I jumped on the opportunity. We agreed on 10:00 until 8:00. I would start with basic training tomorrow and work the whole day. Once track ended I could pick up more hours and learn to work the register, at which point I'd get a raise to $8.50 an hour.

I wanted to hop a ride home with Mom, but without my bike rack there was no way her tiny sedan could carry me, my bike, and groceries. Once home, I flew through my homework knowing that I'd be out with Dad for the rest of the day and working tomorrow. Mom was happy about me getting the job, but reminded me that I'd have to either go to mass at 8:00 in the morning or on Saturday evenings. Agreed. Though I hated going to church, I wasn't going to fight her on this one.

Lois, Dad, and Devon arrived right on time at noon, Layne and I paraded into the hideous wagon, and we were off to Applebee's for lunch. Dad thought this was his birthday lunch, and I guess it was, but he was overjoyed to see the tickets for this afternoon's baseball game in New Britain. The four o'clock start was perfect, that gave us time for lunch, a change to warmer clothes, and batting practice.

You need to understand something: My dad loves baseball. He could watch a game in the Arctic in the dead of winter between two teams from Greenland and be perfectly content. It's amazing we'd never taken him to a ball game for his birthday or father's day before. An added bonus was that though I had intended on paying for everybody's ticket, which would have run 42 dollars, Lois picked up the whole tab saying it was the thought that counted and she wanted me to save my money...plus our father would never know.

The only sour note was on the drive home. Dad asked what we did for Mom for her birthday, I told him the whole story, which he thought was really great of us. Layne even added in how Mark called her at work and had flowers sent there. And therein the problem arose. I guess Dad had just assumed that Mark had been so busy at school and being away, that he had simply allowed their birthdays to slip his mind.

But clearly that wasn't the case. How could he remember Mom's and forget Dad's? They were on the same day.

I knew the answer. Mark was making his anti-Dad statement. I wonder if Dad will retaliate by not sending the tuition in the fall. He won't, but it would be great to see Mark's reaction.

So last night I finished reading *On the Road.* I'm not sure if I fully 'get' the book yet, but I'm on my way to figuring it out. At several points I found myself reading backwards. What I mean by that is sometimes I became confused or lost, so I reread earlier portions of the book to regain my control of what was happening. Last night Mom was shocked when she asked me what page I was on, and my response was a smaller number than the previous hour she asked.

But the book was amazing. Remember how I told you that I can't wait to see where my life takes me and that I want to live everyday to the fullest? Well that's just how Dean Moriarity lives. He's not the main character in the story, but he's the catalyst for most of the action. You see, he's a leader, actually more of a rebel, and lives his life how he wants to. But the narrator, Sal Paradise, seems to follow Dean, desperate to live the same way, but unable to because of too many restrictions that hold him back–most notably himself. Dean, on the other hand, is a free spirit who rejects society's norms and lives each day to the fullest–he is full of passion.

If I say I want to be Dean Moriarity, then I've missed the point. But I also remember what Blackwell said about me following and not leading; Jennifer said it too. Similarly, I also remember Blackwell's plans for me: high school, college, successful job (I think that would make me a follower–irony?).

I don't want to be Dean Moriarity, but I relish in his life's philosophy. I'm happiest when I'm doing the things that make me happy: being myself, running, exploring my own interests and learning about them. My best memories are the day trips we used to take as kids, whether it was to Block Island with my mom, New York with my dad, or Annapolis with my grandparents; I simply loved going to new places. At night before I go to bed, I sometimes flip on the Travel Channel; several times I've found myself postponing sleep to learn about Melbourne's hidden treasures or ghost towns along Route 66. Maps adorn the walls of my bedroom and I own more road atlases than most libraries, though I don't drive yet. I just think maps are cool. Whenever I go someplace new, I bring my camera and snap thousands of photos. I save everyone on my computer and never delete any, even the out of focus ones; they too are a reminder of where I've been. In my wallet, I have a running list of all the places I want to go. They are in no particular order, but I've decided that the Pacific Ocean is first...and I want to go there by train of course.

It's late, real late. I haven't been up past midnight in a long while. I was thinking about how I haven't felt depressed in a while; which is good. I really hope that feeling never comes back. I've heard stories about people who go years without feeling depressed, then it reemerges all over again. Mom also told me about how many teenagers go through it and it was probably just a faze for me. She said if it comes back again to tell her right away instead of after it happens. I think she'll send me to a therapist if it happens again. But I truly believe that I'm happier now because I'm learning to be the person that I envision myself as being and doing the things that I want to do. And those things simply don't include getting wasted on a Saturday night in April. I'm thinking about that right now because Darrin actually invited me to tonight's party. A few months ago I would have felt like I had to be there. But tonight, I don't want to be there, so I'm not. I love that thought process.

I have to be up by seven to make mass, which I'll walk to, then I'll walk to work from there. Mom said she'd pick me up when my shift is over. I can't wait to start. I need money.

April 28, 2002

I figured out why my teachers always preach the value of an education and the importance of having a skill.

The training for my job lasted all of fifteen minutes. In the parking lot, push the carts from the collection area back to the store. When bagging groceries, ask paper or plastic politely. Give the customers what they want: if they want two bags, give them two bags. Package items together: soaps/cleaners, cold products, meats, "soft" products...in other words, don't put the watermelon with the bread or the bleach with the fresh fish. SIMPLE. Any fool could do this job. The wage, true it was low, wasn't being paid for my skill, simply, I was being paid for my time. I knew right away that I was replaceable and that thousands of kids had done this job before me; the sad part were the number of adults on the time sheet–I assume they never finished school or garnered a skill.

True, I intended on doing a good job, but I knew that by the dearth of applicants for menial work that my job was pretty safe.

I actually enjoyed my first day; when I grew tired of simply bagging groceries, I went to the parking lot and retrieved carts. When that became tiresome, I bagged groceries. Sometimes it's neat seeing what people are buying.

Like this one chick, she bought shitloads of groceries, but I remember she also bought condoms and a home pregnancy test. Either poor planning or wishful thinking, I guess.

This other dude, he bought a dozen or so cans of dehydrated peaches. Why? Nothing else, just the peaches.

The other thing I noticed was that I was appreciated. Since only three baggers were scheduled, that meant at best only a third or the cashiers had baggers. They loved it when we came since they didn't have to bag. And so did the customers: it meant a swifter line. And when something went wrong, the cashier had to handle the problem, not me. For instance, this one lady had a shit when her frozen broccoli rang up as $1.49; according to her, it was $1.39. The cashier didn't even bother calling for a price check; she just gave it to her. This lady was foaming at the mouth over a freaking dime.

Dad called after I got home; he said him and Mark had an argument. Apparently Mark called and apologized for 'forgetting' Dad's birthday. Dad called him on the lie.

Dad said he and Mark had a heated discussion on their relationship. Mark and my dad will probably never see eye to eye. I remember what Mom said about Mark knowing what life was like when Dad lived here, and I think that's what still burns him up: he feels abandoned. But I also know that he has it pretty good, Dad does care for him, and supports him financially. It's complicated. And sadly, I don't really care.

April 30, 2002

Blackwell and I had our chat regarding *On the Road.* He told me up-front to overlook the illicit drug use in the conversation and discussion. Funny, I guess he remembered my outlook on *The Basketball Diaries*, however, I had no intentions of bringing it up considering how the book moved me in so many other ways.

We agreed and disagreed often. In fact, I'm not sure if either of us truly knew where the other one stood, let alone ourselves, by the end of lunch.

Blackwell truly understood my perspective regarding Dean and living life to its fullest and his outlook on life. He said he wasn't surprised that I rejoiced in it considering my recent awakenings. But he cautioned me too. Blackwell asked me to note that Dean was never satisfied; all of his relationships eventually fizzled and he was always following a dream that was out of his reach.

My rebuttal was powerful, or so I thought. I reminded Blackwell that Dean didn't care about his failures, he continued to try to live his dream, to be his own person, he never wallowed in defeat.

We came to a mutual truce regarding Dean: He lived life to the fullest while never truly fulfilling his wants and desires. But since it was a truce, I don't think either one of us felt comfortable with it: we both surrendered our central arguments.

Since our conversation regarding *On the Road* engulfed all of lunch, I went back to Blackwell's room right after school. I only had a few minutes since practice was starting early today, but I wanted to get a new book and to just tell him about how things had been going lately.

"*The Great Gatsby* will teach you about green lights, figure it out."

At first glance I was guessing this would have something to do with driving since I was turning 16 in a matter of days, but I had a feeling it wouldn't be. "Thanks Mr. Blackwell, hey, like I said before, it's not going to be like that."

"Come again, Andrew."

"Remember how you said I was heading down the wrong path and was jeopardizing my future? I told you that I wasn't going to do that. I'm not trying to prove you right or wrong, I'm just saying that it's not going to be like that."

"I hope not. Now go to practice and don't get lost chasing squirrels or whatever it is you do out there."

5/3/02

Bennett held me out of today's race. He said that there was nobody in the race today that could run with me and that there was no point doing anything stupid. For May, the weather was ridiculous, cloudy and in the thirties. So instead, he had me do a comfortable distance run on my own prior to the meet.

I ran seven miles as soon as school released and made it back in time for the National Anthem. During my run, it was strange. So many school busses passed me that I quickly lost count. Some just passed me by. A few had classmates of mine screaming my name out the window. Recently I had become famous on the morning announcements. I had won most of the races I was in and even the laymen throughout the school realized my two mile time was fast: most of the student body couldn't run a single mile in that time. In PE class on Wednesday, we had to run the 'gym class mile.' Not that I was showing off, but I jogged a 5:25 mile, by far the best in class, and didn't even breathe hard.

But it was one bus I remember most: it was the voice that I immediately caught, Darrin's. Apparently by not showing up to his party last weekend I had offended him, which was strange since we hadn't hung out since Harris had died.

"You fucking faggot!" he screamed at me.

Luckily for me, the bus stopped about thirty yards up the road at a traffic light and that allowed me the opportunity to pass the bus.

At first, I thought Darrin was kidding, but upon approaching the bus again, I noticed he was ready for me again.

"Run you pansy!"

And this comment set the record straight: Darrin was not joking around with me. For the rest of my run, all I could think about were his comments. I never broke stride and never called anything back to him. I just ran, wondering why he hated me so much. I told him up-front that I wasn't going to the party because I just didn't feel like the partying type anymore. He seemed cool with that. I said it would be cool if we hung out some time and that maybe we could go bowling or something. Darrin responded positively, I thought, and never once during the week did I feel any animosity towards him. I just don't know what happened.

During the meet today, my main job was to shadow Bennett. This job is usually reserved for the injured and/or suspended. My primary responsibility was to assist in timing: split times in relays, lap times in distance races. During the sprints, I was free to do as I pleased.

As the 110 meter high hurdles set to launch, I wandered toward the team area, where Darrin was strumming on a guitar with several of the distance runners. I thought this was odd on so many levels. I'd never seen him at a meet before, this wasn't his usual peer group, and just an hour or so ago he rode past me on the bus screaming obscenities while I ran.

"What's up?" I began. I wasn't looking to pick a fight, but I really wanted to know what was going on between the two of us.

"Nothing," was his only reply as he continued to play.

"Yo, I heard what you said as I went running by earlier."

"So."

"So what's up, what was the point of all of that?"

"Andrew," Darrin began, "lighten up, I was just having a little fun with you, that's all. It was a joke."

"No, it wasn't. You don't have to like me or want to be my friend or anything like that, but that wasn't cool."

I knew Darrin didn't want to have this conversation and I could sense tension in the air as he stopped playing and everybody slowly drifted away from us.

"Andrew," Darrin began again, "you're a fucking weirdo. There, are you happy? I said it. We all feel that way. Me, Chris, Haley, everybody. You don't talk to anyone anymore. You don't hang out anymore. You sit by yourself and read during lunch. Jennifer only comes to see you because she feels bad for you. Fuck Andrew, life goes on and you just sit there mourning Harris' death all by yourself. I tried to be your friend last weekend and you blew me off. Nothing more, I ain't trying again."

"I'm over Harris' death," I wanted to make that point clear, "why do you think I do what I want instead of the very shit you fuckers do that killed him? I learned to do what I want and if that makes me weird so be it. But I don't throw shit at you at lunch like you do to me or scream shit at you. Darrin, I told you it would be cool to hang out, I just don't want to be fucked up when we do. But if that's how you feel about me, then whatever, just leave me alone."

"Fine," and that's all he said as he walked away.

I don't think I'll ever talk to him again. The only thing he said that concerned me was the idea that Jennifer only sat with me because she felt bad. I'm pretty sure it wasn't true, after all, Jennifer doesn't hang with them and we already had that conversation. Part of me wanted to rush over and ask her, but the intelligent side of me took over and noted that she had a big race coming up and I needed to be more secure in trusting the few people who gave me the time of day. I wouldn't let this eat at me. I knew I couldn't because these are the types of things that bring me down and create that sick depressing feeling; which I must overcome.

Before I had too much time to fixate on this, Bennett called me over for the start of the two mile. I assumed he'd have me record lap times, but I was wrong. Instead, he told me to simply watch the top three runners for the whole race and see what they were doing.

Bennett was right, though all three were decent runners, I would've easily won the race today. I'd been consistently down around 10:09. Today, first place was 10:24.

"So," Bennett queried, "what did you notice?"

"Well," actually, I wasn't too sure I noticed anything, "I can beat all of them without trying. But I think the second place dude is going to be a real good runner. I think he's only a freshman, but he has excellent form and seemed to know what he was doing out there today. The winner kept looking over his shoulder like he was scared or something. The third place guy was all over the place with form."

"Yeah, that's right. That guy in second is Wilbon, he's a freshman. He'll be awesome come cross country season. He's just not quite ready yet. Anderson won, he's a junior who runs track to stay in shape for football. He doesn't really care too much, but he has talent. He's not scared, though. He's just not used to winning; it's probably the first race he's ever won and his coach was ecstatic that you weren't running. I didn't even bother looking at the third guy so whatever you said is right," Bennett chortled.

"You think Wilbon's got a chance at going to the State meet? I have to run against him, right?"

"Not this year; he's just not quite there yet. You'll beat him easily this year, but you'll fight him hard the next couple of years. He'll kick your ass if you show up for cross country like you did last year."

"I'll be in shape, coach."

"I know."

5/4/02

Practice starts in an hour or so; but I haven't slept all night. You see, there's a huge part of me that wants to call Jennifer and find out if she only comes and visits me at lunch because she feels sorry for me. But I know I can't do that for so many reasons. I'm scared of succumbing to this fear. This is the sickly feeling I've been trying to fight for so long. I've been comfortable with myself for a few months now, but this I can't handle. For some reason Jennifer is different. True, we don't hang out that often, but knowing that she's my friend means everything to me. In my mind, I know that Jennifer hates the sick, depressed Andrew. It drove her away from me. By asking Jennifer about Darrin's accusation would only reinforce her beliefs. But if they were true, they would destroy me.

I sucked at practice today.

5/6/02

Strangely, I think work really helped me out yesterday. I noticed how pathetic the vast majority of the customers were. Rich stuck up snobs who live vicariously through their children arguing over the price of oranges. Folks on food stamps buying lottery tickets and cigarettes–pathetic. And as I saw these people, I kept telling myself how lucky I am.

At lunch today, I made a point of sitting at Jennifer's table and communicating with not only her, but also her friends. I felt better than on Saturday, but still not as good as I did up until Darrin's confrontation. But I made a point of putting on a good face–not too much, you know, not phony, but enough so that everyone thought I was happy go lucky. I think it worked; just before lunch ended, Jennifer said we should hangout this weekend.

It's amazing, though she didn't say what we should do, her mere suggestion, not mine, completely changed my outlook. I felt great! I knew she didn't just feel sorry for me, but enjoyed my company.

But then I realized it, I have so far to go to overcome my demons. I'm just thankful that Mom worked Saturday and I worked Sunday, otherwise she might've noticed and sent me off to therapy.

5/8/02

Today was the last tune-up race before the district meet. Sanderson of Griswold beat me. He ran a 9:59; I ran a 10:05. I'm not disappointed in my time, but there's quite an issue at stake. If I win my district, then I automatically qualify for States. But if I don't win the district, then I have to run under 10:00 flat. Sanderson is in my district. Luckily, Weaver isn't. Sanderson, though, is going to be an issue. Six seconds is a lot to make up in ten days. Districts is on May 17th, Saturday, I must find a way to qualify. I've come too far to give up, and worked too hard to let myself down.

On the bus ride home, Bennett told me to stay focused and not worry about it, but the truth to the matter is that I am worried. I think he is too. Rather than having one of our intimate coach-runner conversations that we'd both taken to, he simply told me to relax and sit with the team. My guess, he didn't know what to tell me and needed time to devise a plan. All I can do is come to practice tomorrow and work my butt off.

5/10/02

Today marks my sixteenth birthday.

Usually Mom has our birthday presents sitting on the table when we get up in the morning, but not today. In fact, Mom was sound asleep when I awoke and still in bed when I hopped out of the shower. I figured she'd had a long week and was exhausted. No big deal. Just as I was finishing breakfast, she emerged and asked if I had anything going on after school today. I assumed this was to help plan my birthday dinner or something like that. I remembered that Jennifer had said she wanted to do something this weekend, but I didn't know what, where, and when. So I simply told Mom that I had no definite plans.

With that, she went to take a shower and I left for school. I found it odd that she didn't wish me a happy birthday, but I figured she was plotting something for later today.

I think most of my 'old' friends still knew it was my birthday, but they chose to ignore it. I guess I would too if I were in their shoes. After all, Darrin had made it clear that I was weird and clearly none of them were my friends anymore.

Jennifer, on the other hand, surprised me. I expected her to say happy birthday, but I wasn't expecting her to greet me with a hug and a gift as I walked into the cafeteria for lunch. I should point out that we had eaten lunch together everyday this week. Much of my doing too. In fact, I'd sat at her table every day and actually enjoyed it. Considering she sat with all girls, plus me, the ego trip helped a little. An added bonus was that even Darrin and his gang wouldn't throw shit at me, I guess out of fear they might miss and hit one of the ladies. Or perhaps they were jealous? Me, the 'weirdo' was sitting with the girls and they weren't. True, several girls had joined them a few weeks back, but I noticed that their table had dwindled to just a bunch of guys again, oh well.

I didn't know if I should open the gift now or later, so I was going to ask Jennifer, but I could tell by the bounce in her step that she wanted me to open it now. Though the box was big, it was remarkably light–I had no clue what she could've gotten me.

Tickets. Two of them to be exact, for Radiohead in New Haven–tonight. By far one of my favorite bands and I knew they were playing tonight. But going to the show had never crossed my mind because tickets were expensive and I had no one to go with. Though I didn't mind doing certain things on my own, I never envisioned myself alone at a concert. I guess that would make me just too much of a loser.

I simply hugged Jennifer to show my appreciation and I knew that the other ticket was obviously for her.

I couldn't believe it. Not only did Jennifer want to hangout with me, but she also wanted to make me happy.

After school, but before practice, I took a moment to myself in the locker room. I knew I was falling for Jennifer again. Actually, I wasn't falling for her, I'd already accomplished that. But a large part of me started to believe that she was falling for me. I didn't want to spoil it like I did last time. I made a pact with myself to be the person that I envision myself as being–happy, original, spontaneous, spirited. I like that person; that is me.

After practice, I went home and was surprised to see Mom home already. She barely acknowledged me as I walked through the door, but just before I took my post practice shower, I told her I was going to New Haven with Jennifer to see a concert.

"That's fine Andrew, what do you want on your pizza?"

"I don't care, anything's good for me."

I must admit, I found it quite strange that nobody had wished me a happy birthday except for Jennifer and her friends, but I still figured Mom had something up her sleeve.

But dinner was just me, Mom, and Layne, plus a cheese, mushroom, sausage, and pepperoni pizza. No birthday cake. No presents. Nothing.

Mom said she would drop me off at the train station at 7:30, but strangely I declined, I was sort of looking forward to the 20 minute walk, especially on such a nice night and it still being light out and all. Jennifer's parents said they'd drop me off after we got back from the show. Just before seven as I was preparing to leave for the train–I didn't want to be late nor did I want Jennifer to have to wait for me–the phone rang. I thought it was going to be Dad. He usually called around this time and since it was my birthday I assumed it was his obligatory call. Though I wouldn't see him until next weekend, he was always good about calling me for special occasions, especially birthdays and holidays. It wasn't. A telemarketer on a Friday, talk about pathetic.

While taking the train to New Haven, I told Jennifer how I thought my parents forgot my birthday, especially Mom. Strangely, it didn't really bother me. Though I was disappointed, the only person who I would want to spend my birthday with, Jennifer, also wanted to spend it with me. She was sitting right next to me, having chosen to remember, having chosen to be with me, knowing she was making me happy.

The show was awesome. Radiohead played a really long set hitting on old songs, new songs, popular songs, obscure songs, etc. I know Jennifer likes Radiohead, but there were definitely times she was at a loss for the tune they were playing.

Our train home didn't leave until 11:30, so we had a few minutes to dart into a diner and grab a couple of milkshakes to go. Of all things, Jennifer produced a candle from her purse and lit it to sing happy birthday to me.

Sitting next to her on the train, I noticed she was tiring, I simply put my arm around her, kissed her on the forehead, and said thank you. With that, she leaned on me, using my body as her pillow. Something told me we'd be together again soon.

5/11/02

About one o'clock this afternoon, Mom came bursting into my room with the mail; in it was a card addressed to me from my godmother, obviously it was a birthday card.

"Oh my Andrew," Mom began, "I forgot all about yesterday being your birthday. I'm so sorry. I feel terrible. Oh son, you must think I'm the worst mother in the world. And after what you and Layne did for my birthday. I'm so sorry Andrew."

"It's alright Mom, shit happens."

"Andrew, I didn't forget all together. I do have your present. Hold on, let me run into my room and get it for you."

While Mom searched for my present, I opened my godmother's card: the usual, a corny cartoon card and a ten dollar bill. It's the thought that counts.

Licking the envelope shut, Mom burst back into my bedroom handing me my birthday present. Still wet with her saliva, I undid her handiwork quite quickly. Usually my Mom's cards are just as inane as my godmother's, but not this year. Instead, Mom's card was quite poetic, I won't bore you with the lineage, but the essence included the days of happiness that I have brought her and the eternal love she feels for me. I could tell that Mom spent a lot of time picking it out and had planned this card carefully, of course the irony being that she forgot my actual birthday. Inside the card was a receipt. For an instant, I thought she forgot to throw away the drugstore record, but upon further inspection I discovered that the receipt was for driver's education classes. Though swearing up and down for a year that she wouldn't pay for driver's education and that if I wanted to drive I'd better get a job, Mom caved and gave it to me for my birthday.

"What about that whole getting a job thing," I questioned.

"Andrew, I'm so proud of what you're doing right now. You're doing great in school, working, staying out of trouble, and obviously the star of the track team. I know I was really hard on you a few months ago. I know you've lost most of your friends, but I've never been more proud of you. And I wanted you to know that. I can't tell you how sorry I am that I missed your birthday yesterday, but I wanted to give you something that you truly wanted and to show you that I do love you tremendously."

"Thanks Mom. I love you too."

"I know son. There's a catch though. You must keep being successful. This isn't a one time thing. After you get your license, I'm going to give you my old car because I need a new one with all the miles I drive for work."

"REALLY!" I couldn't believe Mom was going to give me her car. True, it was no prize, a 1995 Dodge, but I couldn't believe Mom was going to let me have it.

"The catch, Andrew, is that you will pay your insurance, that's why you're working. And, if you're grades fall off or you start getting into trouble, the car will go the way of the junkyard. Clear."

"Absolutely. Thanks Mom!"

5/12/02

By the time work rolled around today, I had all but given up on my father remembering it was my birthday, after all, it was two days later. He does call every Sunday, but I had a feeling it would be another normal conversation ending with him being 'just a phone call away.'

My shift was strange; mostly because so many people were working. In fact, pretty much every register had a bagger, so not only did that limit my escapades to the parking lot to escape from the doldrums of 'paper or plastic,' but it also meant that I no longer had to bounce between two and three registers when I was bagging. For pretty much the entire shift I was working with Forrest, a kid who seemed about my age.

As the shift progressed, we started to talk casually, during a slow time and price checks, turns out he lives right near the beach that I frequent. But he goes to a private school in the next town over; he doesn't want to, but his parents make him. My town has a reputation for having superior public schools, so very few high schoolers from town attend private school. Forrest said that most of his friends live in other towns since so few kids from town go to his school, The Sound Preparatory Academy.

During our shift, we revealed who we really were. I told him about my 'old' friends and how now I pretty much keep to myself, run, and hangout with Jennifer. I told him about Harris' death; he had heard about it since it was all over the news, but didn't know him at all. Forrest spoke about how so many of the kids at his school came from filthy rich families who just wasted all of their parents' money. He wasn't like that, or so he claimed. True, he said, that his family was pretty wealthy, but his parents wouldn't give him money, they made him earn it like everybody else. I guess that's why he was working the register at the local grocery store. He told me that he too didn't have tons of friends. According to Forrest, he hung out with the same two dudes pretty much all of the time.

Turns out we like the same music and do the same things in the summer–hangout at the beach and play volleyball. Everyday during the summer you can find me playing beach volleyball and working on my perfect tan. Well, I don't know if that will be true this summer; my beach volleyball team has all but disbanded with Harris' death and my termination from the group. Forrest said he thought I looked familiar from the courts. Apparently he and his buddies had wrestled up a fourth friend from time to time and played on the courts throughout the summer. Quite honestly, I'd played so many games the past summers that I could barely remember any face from the crowd.

True, it was only May and the water was still too cold for swimming, but the beach was starting to warm up and the courts were ready for play; I hadn't been there yet because I had no one to hang with. Forrest said he and his two buds were looking for a fourth and he thought it would be cool if I played with them next weekend. I told him that I had districts for track on Saturday, but practice would be cancelled on Friday so I could get a couple games in after school. Suddenly, I was in danger of making not just one friend, Forrest, but if all went well two more.

That day at work we started playing a game with the customers. Forrest's job was to say absolutely nothing to the customers. My job was to do the exact opposite of whatever the customer asked for.

The first victim was truly pathetic; some older guy wearing golf clothes who was clearly returning to town for the first time since his six month hiatus in Florida.

"Hello, sir how are you," I greeted, "would you like paper or plastic?'

"Paper only," he retorted, "I hate plastic, kills the birds you know."

Immediately I started shuffling his groceries into plastic bags as he fumbled through his pockets for his store card (not used since Thanksgiving) and coupons. He didn't notice me ignoring his orders. Finally, Forrest finished scanning the order, took the man's coupons, and merely pointed at the computer screen in front of him.

After paying, the man looked at his carriage full of plastic and nearly exploded like a firecracker misfired from a barge on Independence Day. "PAPER, I wanted only paper, I hate plastic!" the man screamed at me.

"I'm very sorry sir," I feigned, "I could've sworn you said plastic only."

Forrest just grinned, but he couldn't make any noise, otherwise he'd lose the game. I immediately pulled out paper bags and started placing his plastic bags inside of the paper bags.

"No, get rid of the plastic all together," the red faced man two toned.

By this point I had all of his plastic inside of paper and had grown 'frustrated' with his unrealistic demands. At a loss, I dumped all of his groceries on the counter and said "fine, you do it."

Irrate, the man didn't know what to do as I walked two registers down to the only cashier lacking a bagger. I kept looking back at Forrest as he bagged the man's groceries in paper. Forrest never said a word. Sure, he gestured with his body and face, but he never spoke.

After the man left, I returned to Forrest's register. He called me a motherfucker for my stunt, but acknowledged it was well played. I couldn't believe he stayed silent, but he said since the guy never stopped complaining, he never had to respond.

I think Forrest and I are going to be friends. That would be cool to have a friend again.

About 8:45 Dad called. It was a normal conversation...school, track, life. I told him about the district race coming up and that I could go to the State Championship. He attempted to be interested and said he would try to make it.

I reminded Dad that the day of his race was his day and that we could leave straight from the race if he wanted to. I think that struck a spark with him since he realized the race was in Middletown and he wouldn't have to drive all the way to my house to meet me. I don't know, he'll probably find some excuse not to watch me run in circles.

"Well pal, I'm just a phone call away," he started to conclude.

But I wouldn't let him. I was pissed at him. As much as I understood Mom forgetting my birthday, then accepting her apology. I couldn't accept Dad forgetting my birthday. Christ, it was now the eleventh and my birthday was on the ninth. Plus, I'd organized a great day at the ball yard for his birthday, and he'd forgotten mine–not to mention his own anger about Mark forgetting his birthday, though that was intentional.

"Hey Dad," I began, "you know I just turned 16 on Friday."

"Andrew, oh my, that's right, and I haven't forgotten. Lois and I were waiting to see you on Saturday so we could celebrate."

"But you didn't even call. I thought you were just a phone call away?"

"Well, Friday was hectic at work and I didn't get home until very late."

"Oh, well, I was around all day yesterday too, Dad," I was trying to pick a fight, which was unlike me, but I wanted to hear my father admit to his shortcoming, but he wouldn't.

"Well son, like I said, Lois and I have a great day planned for you on Saturday."

"Ok, I'll see you on Saturday then." For some reason I was letting him off the hook and I didn't know why.

But then he put himself right back on it. "Is there anything special you want for your birthday or something you want to do?"

"Dad," I said, "I thought you and Lois had it all planned out?"

"Well, well, we do," he lied, "we just wanted to make sure we did what you wanted to, Andrew."

"Watch me run on Saturday."

"You got it. We'll be there."

It bothered me that I had to ask that of my father. I'm not even sure if I wanted him there. Especially since I was fully aware of the fact that I may come up short of my goal of qualifying for the State Championship, but that was a risk I was clearly ready to take.

Suddenly, for the first time in my life, I understood Mark.

5/16/02

Today at practice, Bennett called me aside to discourse the upcoming district race. As I had expected, there would be no practice tomorrow, so he wanted to talk race strategy today. Unlike the previous few weeks, Bennett spoke to me very little at practice. Being the over thinker that I am, I devised several plausible explanations for this. One, Bennett didn't want to make me nervous or over think the race. Two, Bennett didn't think I could beat Sanderson and I was too far away still to break ten minutes, thus not qualifying for States, and he didn't want to break it to me. Three, Bennett had no clue how to get me into States.

I think it was a combination of all three.

"I've been thinking about your two mile all week Andrew. And here's the thing, you either have to beat Sanderson or break ten minutes."

"I know coach," his beginning this way made me feel real stupid–I've known this for a long time, but I guess he still wasn't sure what he wanted to say to me.

"If you try beating Sanderson, you may fall into a trap and end up running his race, which you know is a bad thing. You have to always run your race. I hope you've learned that this year kid."

"Definitely, I remember what happened to Jenkevich at Middletwon."

"Right, exactly. But I'm worried that if I give you time goals that it could hurt you. You've got to drop just over five seconds, and that's a lot. I don't want to put you in a position that you could've beaten Sanderson, but didn't because of a time goal–then you run the risk of losing and not qualifying."

"I know."

"So," Bennett began, "I wanted you to be involved in creating the race strategy. If you want to run a race that beats Sanderson, then you need to go home and devise a workable plan to accomplish that. Tonight I'm going home to create several different lap time scenarios that will bring you under ten flat. Go home tonight; think about how you want to run the race, then we'll go with it on Saturday. I'll be prepared either way."

"Alright, I'll let you know."

A trillion thoughts ran through my head simultaneously. The most vivid was the memory of Mom leaving the newspaper clipping at the breakfast table after my first major victory. That was the morning I set a goal of going to States. I truly believed that I had never lost focus of that goal: I've been working hard, paying attention, and trying to learn more about the sport.

"Coach," I called as Bennett walked away from me following our conversation, "I know the answer already."

"What is it."

"I'm going to beat Sanderson by running my race. I know how to do it."

"Are you sure?"

" Yes. You taught me," I added the last line not only because it was mostly true, but also because I wanted to stroke Bennett's ego a little.

"How?"

"Sanderson likes to run up front and lead early. I'm going to let him do that. But his second mile always slows. He gets tired. Your lap times have been designed to keep me from tiring. I'm going to trail him for the first mile. Then let my endurance take over. I'll beat him during the second mile and kick early, real early if I have to."

"I can see that. You've got to hold yourself to that Andrew, you can't let Sanderson get too big of a lead because you'll kill yourself catching up and have nothing for your kick."

"True, but I need you to do something for me coach. I've always been good at focusing on what I have to do–making lap time times, passing at the right points, but I'm terrible about focusing on form. I'm going to need every extra edge possible on Saturday. Yell at me the second I tighten up, keep my eyes forward, remind me about my stride–even if I'm doing it right, it'll keep me from forgetting."

"You got it," Bennett smiled.

"Thanks coach."

"Hey Andrew, you can do this. I know you can."

I found Bennett's choice of pronoun interesting. Earlier in the season he switched from 'you' to 'we' symbolically showing me that my success was tied to him as well. That he wanted to work with me to achieve my goals and that he believed in me. But he's always told me that I must run my race and that he can't help me once the gun goes off. Either I do it, or I don't. Bennett switching back to 'you' let me know that he'd be there to support me, but I had to be the one to make the plan come to fruition. And he was certainly right about that.

5/17/02

It rained all day today; practice was cancelled as I had anticipated, and I had nothing to do. Forrest called me to say that volleyball was definitely out, but they were hitting up the bowling alley after dinner. Though it would be cool to hangout with people again, I declined citing my impending race early the next morning. He said he'd forgotten all about that and he'd catch me at work on Sunday.

A small, very small part of me wish I didn't have to run tomorrow, not because I was scared or disliked running, but because I really wanted friends again. And though Jennifer was great, I had no 'boys' to hang with anymore. But in time, all things come, and as Mom says, it's good to want things.

With the big race being tomorrow, I know that I must have a tranquil night; similarly, I know that sleep will not come easily. Not that reading puts me to sleep, in fact, I've grown to love reading, but reading relaxes me, it allows me to escape from the anxious thoughts that plague my mind, and in time, comforts me, allowing to me calm myself, and tonight, perhaps, even sleep.

For the first time since Blackwell gave it to me, I picked up *The Great Gatsby*. And I can't put it down. Blackwell told me to understand the green light, and almost immediately I picked up on the title character convulsing toward a green light across the dock from Nick's (the narrator's) dock, the dock of his second cousin, the dock where he dined that very same night. But I'm still trying to figure out what it means.

...I read on. Colors are intensely present throughout the novel...yellow, gray, white. I remember Blackwell's endless diatribes on color and symbolism, now I'm trying to remember what they mean. White–pure, gray–dying/desperate, green–go, but yellow, I don't know, time to keep reading.

...So here it is. Green must mean go. Yeah, it's almost midnight and I read the whole book. Still lost on yellow, but I've got the rest. White is purity or goodness. Throughout the story Daisy (she's the lost girl) is searching for that which is pure, but somewhere along the way she became corrupted. Gray is death and decay. The Valley of Ashes, from the story, are in gray, and here, all things die and there is no rebirth. Green is go, but more than that. It's the American dream, everything I've been searching for. Gatsby sought the American dream, but he failed, just what is Blackwell trying to tell me? He told me to pay attention to the green light. Obviously, Blackwell is disturbed by my 'destiny philosophy.' I believe in following my dreams and doing only that which makes me happy–existentialism? Perhaps. But I also know that there are certain things I must do, contrary to existentialist thought. I must do well in school, otherwise I can't run track or cross country. But perhaps doing what I must will also allow me to do what I want.

Though I read tonight, I still can't sleep. The race is tomorrow, I can't believe how nervous I am. I have the plan to beat Sanderson, but carrying it out is a whole new scenario. Plus, I'm still stuck on that whole green light thing. I guess I just have to go for it, just like Gatsby, even if I fail.

5/18/02

And the gun went off.

One lap into the race, I heard the call of 65, obviously Sanderson was running the race I expected; he was out early and trying to win the two mile during the first mile. I had to find a way to withstand his onslaught. This was my fastest opening lap of the season, but I needed to be fast to qualify for the State championship. I hadn't broken ten minutes all season and I'd never beaten Sanderson. I must do something different.

For a split second, I thought about playing Sanderson's game. I was on his heels at the end of the first lap. I considered passing him and forcing him to run with me. I pulled along side of him, but quickly sank back. My race, not his, I thought to myself. Running my race meant trailing him for a mile, then winning on the second mile. If I passed him on lap two of eight, I risked exhausting myself, allowing Sanderson to win and me falling short of my sub-ten minute goal.

But perhaps pulling even sent a message; I think I scared Sanderson, for he took off a little and seemed to be running harder on lap two than on lap one. I wasn't scared yet; I knew I needed to keep him close, but he wouldn't run away from me on lap two.

At the one mile mark, Sanderson was probably two seconds in front of me; I heard the timer call 4:58 as I passed the line. Theoretically, that would leave me in good shape, even if I didn't beat

Sanderson. If I could keep this pace going, I would run a 9:56 and easily qualify for States. But I was worried; my best time all year was a 10:05 and my fastest first mile time was a 5:01; a part of me felt I was in grave trouble and I was starting to feel spent.

"Look-up! Open up your hands ANDREW!" For the first time, Bennett's screams pierced my train of thought. It was a needed scream. I knew Bennett was confident in my plan and he promised me that he would leave it on my shoulders to carry it out. However, he would watch my form and breathing; he would remind me of what to do and yell at me when I was out of kilter.

Immediately, I looked up and saw Sanderson pulling away from me. This wasn't how it was supposed to happen. Generally speaking, Sanderson fades during the second mile, I should be gaining on him if my plan was going to work out. But I opened my hands, felt my chest and lungs relax, and felt a second wind coming.

By the start of the seventh lap, my shadow had crept nearly face to face with Sanderson's. This is how I imagined it. Two laps for the glory. Might I add, during the last two laps Bennett was great. He walked the opposite direction of the race so that he could see me twice on each lap. And he let me have it all four times. Screaming at me to loosen up, breathe, relax, and to raise my eyes. It was exactly what I needed. He never yelled race strategy. That was my job: to win or lose by; I had earned that privilege. Bennett gave me the structure and form.

With two laps left, I recalled my experiences against the Bethel Public runner, I went with 500 meters to go instead of 400; I out kicked him and won. But Sanderson was also a cross country runner like me, I knew he'd have decent stamina. Yet, Sanderson's track record seemed to suggest that his would fade too. With 600 meters to go, I stopped looking forward. Instead, I looked to my right and caught Bennett's eyes. He seemed to read my mind. Nodding his head in the affirmative direction, Bennett completed my thought. Rather than screaming directions at me, he simply nodded this time. 600 meters to go.

I passed Sanderson with just under 600 meters to go, a little sooner than I had envisioned, but also still within the framework of my plan. I had come this far, I must finish what I had started.

The bell sounded, one lap to go. Bennett stood at the line, silent. It was my race to win or lose. He simply watched; there was nothing else he could yell at me.

By the 200 meter mark, I was feeling it hard, harder than I had ever felt it during any race at any point in my life. My lungs were shot, my legs were Jell-0, my arms were limbs full of cement. And I could see Sanderson's shadow out of the corner of my eye.

Part of me wondered how could Sanderson still be with me; I should've blown him away by now. Part of me knew I was done and he'd overtake me, sending me home in defeat. Part of me longed to hear Bennett's screams that would rejuvenate me. But those were all parts of me. The majority of me decided to fight back. I started with my hands. Open, they were. Next, my stride; knees high, follow through heel to rear. I did. Chest and arms: forward, relaxed, create a regular breathing pattern. I was. These three elements were in line already, there was no extra advantage they would provide me. But part four was obviously out of whack.

If I could see Sanderson's shadow, I was clearly looking in the wrong direction. Immediately I lifted my eyes and as I angled through the last turn, passing the 110 meter line, I began to straighten my body. Directly in front of me would be the finish line. I would look at it and concentrate on it; nothing else.

As my body straightened and I could see the line directly in front of me, out of the corner of my right eye I could see Bennett pantomiming a trampoline artist. No worries; he'd come down just fine. In my mind, I imagined myself darting down the last 100 meters gracefully, lithely to the cheers of the crowd, though in reality, I assume I staggered down the back straightaway ungainly and awkwardly. So long as I won the race, though, it didn't matter.

With about 25 or 30 meters to go, the wall finally hit me. My stomach failed me. I could feel vomit forming in my lungs and it seemed as though my chest was miles in front of my leaded legs. I decided I was close enough to the finish where breathing no longer mattered. Inhaling, or exhaling for that matter, meant that I would certainly lose any and everything my body was holding. Instead, I clasped my lips shut and counted the meters backwards in my head to the finish line.

Illusive and swaying, certain I was going to fall, I watched my right toe cross the finish line; true I was looking down instead of up, but at this point it didn't matter. I opened my mouth, nearly puked, and would've fallen if it wasn't for the finish line judge who grabbed hold of me. Flailing away at his chest, I waited a second or two for my legs to lose their elasticity. The judge congratulated me by name, which surprised me seeing as I'd never seen him before. Anyway, he guided me to the finish line shoot, let me go, and left me to stand aimlessly for several seconds.

While waiting for the clerk to remove my race bib, I hung on for life and death to the ropes of the shoot. I glanced up at the scoreboard and could see the unofficial results already being posted. My name ran first, with a time of 9 minutes and 56.3 seconds. Nearly nine seconds faster than my best race ever, I had won and broken ten minutes. Beneath my name, in second place, read Sanderson's name: 9:56.8. A half second behind me: one step, at most, two steps. I turned to congratulate him and saw that he too was barely holding on to consciousness.

I don't know why, but I hugged him. And he hugged me back. For the first few seconds of our embrace, we were both silent. But then the finish line clerk screamed at me to come forward so she could recognize my victory. I held onto Sanderson for a second or two more, then uttered, "Great race, see you next week."

"Hell yeah, you were great man," Sanderson breathlessly replied.

After being released from the shoot, Bennett simply hugged me. He said nothing, at least at first. Then, as he let me go, I saw tears in his eyes, he grabbed my shoulder and said, "You did it, I'm so proud of you. You did it kid."

On the awards' platform, I listened to the announcer call Dryden's name for third, a bronze, but his 10:07 wasn't good enough for States. Sanderson came next, he took his silver and invitation to the State meet. Finally my name. A gold medal and invitation to the State championship meet. To my right, I could hear my teammates and coaches cheering. To my left, I heard a strange whistle and turned to it. It was my father, mother, step-mother, and two brothers–Layne and Devin, hooting and hollering at the top of their lungs. How strange it was to see my whole family, minus Mark, standing together, a sight I'd never seen before.

Then it occurred to me, Mark would be home in three days, he'd see me run at States. I hadn't come to grips with my feelings towards him yet, and I wasn't sure if I welcomed his return, but I was beginning to understand him and I thought that I could do him proud in another week.

But for now, I was going to stand on the awards' platform and smile like a fool while the crowd cheered and I received my gold medal.

After the meet was over, my dad took me up to his house to celebrate my birthday from last week. According to him, he had the whole day planned, but still wanted to know what I wanted to do. Interesting.

By the time I showered and changed, it was already past noon and I was starving. The cool part was that Dad had prepared for that by firing up the grill with some nice steaks and corn on the cob.

Lunch was awesome.

After we gorged ourselves on the porch, Dad produced a present that looked like a wrapped shoe box. Greedily, I tore through the wrapping and discovered a shoe box, though way too light to contain shoes. Inside, was a gift card to a local hiking store and a map of the Appalachian trail through Connecticut.

"We're going hiking!" Dad proclaimed, "but first you're getting a new pair of hiking boots; I didn't know your size so I figured we'd stop for boots first."

I have to say, this was pretty cool, I loved the outdoors and going for a hike sounded great. My only fear being blisters from new boots and sore legs from today's race; but I was psyched nonetheless.

Our first stop were boots; luckily the salesman had the foresight to realize we were immediately going hiking and reminded us to take it easy–plus he scored an additional sale by suggesting these expensive hiking socks, I still had plenty on my gift card and told him to throw in three more for the family–me plus Dad, Lois, and Devin.

My step mom loves the outdoors, not so much Dad. He's active and all, but he'd rather be shooting hoops in the driveway than fly-fishing on a lake. Yet, he enjoys looking at nature. I guess you could say it's a compromise; I'd like to hike Yellowstone and swim beneath Niagra Falls, my dad would rather drive through Yellowstone and watch me swim from the shore.

Anyways, it was quite a drive to the trail head in Salisbury, we drove through towns in Connecticut that I'd never heard of–Colebrook, Norfolk, and Canaan–each one smaller and more rural than the next. It's amazing how just a matter of a few miles separates city life, suburban life, and rural life. Throughout the drive, I split my time from gawking at the locals to charting a hike that would be suitable for everybody. After an hour or so, we reached the trail head, modestly marked off the side of the road, though numerous parked cars indicated we wouldn't be alone on our hike today.

It was already approaching three o'clock and the Mid-May sun wasn't as strong in the rural northwest corner of the state as it was in the southern part, I was glad Dad insisted on bringing wind breakers. The four of us embarked upon our hiking not knowing really what to expect. As soon as we began, a small stand stopped us, worn, wooded, and weary, containing many pages and a pen at its base. A little card indicated this was a travel log and passerbys were asked to add their real names and trail names. I'd heard about these before in social studies class, but had never seen one in person before. I purposely placed myself fourth in line so I'd have time to think of my trail name; I wanted something spiritual, cool, philosophical, and not dorky.

Approaching the stand, I laughed at my family's names: "Lady Lois," "Old Man Walking," and "the Devonator" appeared before me. Finally, I scrolled "Journey Seeker." Though it wasn't nearly as spiritual, cool, or philosophical as I'd hoped, it did express my truest feelings about life; I was seeking a journey.

The hike itself was relatively uneventful. Mostly a mix of narrow paths, short uphills and downhills, streams, and an occasional overlook of a residence. Not knowing the day's plan, I hadn't brought a camera, luckily Lois had and she promised copies of every picture. Recently, photography had become one of my favorite hobbies, a nice compliment to running, playing guitar, reading, and an having an obsession with trains. Several times I'd taken photographs of the sun rising and setting at the beach, most of them were pasted on my bedroom wall next to the passing shot of express and commuter trains. Lois' photographs would add nicely to the mural.

By the time we made it back to the car, my legs were real sore from all of the activity, but luckily my feet avoided blisters and a long distance run before mass and work would be the remedy for the rest. Dad suggested driving directly back to Mom's house since it was already getting late and we could grab some dinner in town; a quick bite was all that was needed and we all small talked for the next couple of hours.

Despite my entire family forgetting my birthday this year, it turned out to be the best birthday I've ever had.

5/19/02

I have never been so sore in my life. Climbing out of bed was an arduous task to say the least, I think I made it to my feet in just under eleven minutes. Clad in my Simpsons' boxers, I contemplated my morning run. I knew I needed it, I knew it was probably good for me; I dreaded the thought of stretching and feeling every muscle in body rejecting any form of movement. A large chunk of me just wanted to let it go–hey, I made States, that was my goal. But a larger part of me wanted to run well at States and running today would certainly help accomplish that goal.

My trek through the neighborhood was slower than normal. I barely worked up a sweat by the end of the first two miles and I certainly wasn't breathing hard. But with every stride, I could feel my muscles slowly warming up and relaxing. By the end of the seven mile jaunt, I was cruising at a decent pace and thanked myself for listening to my mind, and not my body, earlier in the morning.

Work was no picnic, though it was cool to work with Forrest and recant my district championship, every moment on my feet was cumbersome and pushing carriages in the parking lot felt uphill all day. At a couple of points I wondered how awful I would've felt had I not stretched and ran earlier, but it was irrelevant, I felt awful either way.

One additional bright spot was Jennifer; she dropped by the store just to congratulate me. Though she was at the meet, her qualifying time wasn't good enough to run in an event, therefore she had to sit in the stands away from the competitors. Since I left early with Dad to celebrate my birthday, I never saw Jennifer after the race. Apparently she called last night while I was out with my dad, but clearly Mom had failed to relay the message, typical. The last time Layne and Mom actually delivered a message meant for me occurred when I was in middle school, it was the school calling letting my parents know I skipped class. But I digress. I told Jennifer I was looking forward to track being over so we could hangout more. Though this was certainly a good weekend, it flew by and every minute of the weekend was consumed by things I had to do, which I guess was contrary to my new found existentialist based philosophy, yet it didn't bother me as I enjoyed that which I was doing. In any event, it was cool that Jennifer stopped by. She is half of my peer group now.

5/21/02

I think Bennet let me have Monday to bask in the limelight. My head was pretty much in the clouds all day. During home room, the morning announcements proclaimed my accomplishment and to cheer me on for the state championship. All of my teachers congratulated me, and so did most of the other kids I sat next to in class. Funny thing was, none of those kids were my friends. So while they all wished me good luck for State's, I knew none of them would be there nor would they care either way if I won or lost.

Strangely, I don't think I really care. My goal for the season was to qualify for State's. I had done that. Emotionally and physically I was drained; I couldn't imagine running another race right now. Yet, I had just a few days to go before running against the absolute best competition in the state. True, I didn't want to embarrass myself and finish dead last, minutes behind, but I really didn't care about my place. I guess it's the whole cliche, it's just an honor to be there. Winning? Not possible, at least six guys in the race could blow me away–I have no false illusions about that.

Today, though, was a different story. School was the same as ever. I floated anonymously through my classes, ate with Jennifer and her friends, and went to practice. One girl sprinter, and two boys–javelin and pole vault–also qualified for State's. Just the four of us at practice.

Monday was peaceful and easy. Not today. I guess I was just going through the motions of stretching, and Bennett lit into me. Something about focus and pulled muscles mixed with the biggest race of my life. So much for the jocund spirit that had developed. Stretching became a silent activity.

Since I was the only distance runner, Bennett did give me the courtesy of explaining why he delivered his diatribe during stretching. The only conclusion I could draw was that my success was closely intertwined with his success (which I guess it was) and I wasn't to embarrass him on Saturday.

"Okay Andrew," Bennett began, "you need to set both a place and time goal for Saturday."

Out of the six districts, a total of 16 guys had qualified for State's. It would be a crowded field.

"Well, I know I can't beat the top six. And I'm thinking that I'm probably more beat-up than Sanderson. He only came down a couple of seconds, I came down a lot. I don't think I can beat him again. I really don't have my legs back yet."

"To be expected, Andrew. But also remember that the strong competition will give you a little boost plus the race is still a few days off."

"I know," I pondered, "I think I can finish eighth, and that would be cool to be in the top half. As far as time, I don't know. It will be hard for me to pick a guy to run with since more than half of the field I've never ran against. But I was thinking just breaking ten would put me at the very rear of the field, probably thirteenth or even worse."

"Yeah, ten minutes flat will be last or second to last place."

"Coach, I don't know if I can run a 9:52, but I'm gonna give it every last ounce I got."

"Then stop acting like a moron Andrew." This line caught me off guard. Here we were having a pleasant conversation, and the next thing I know, Bennett is all over me again.

"Come again," is all I could reply.

"You had your day or two to celebrate and be the toast of the school. Now, you have to work again. Nobody goes to the Superbowl to lose, they go to win. Track's a little different, instead of two teams, you got sixteen. But you go to win, or at the very least give it everything you have. Don't just be happy to be there. Get your head out of the clouds and start training. You only have four days to prepare, don't waste them."

"Got it. Why the attitude, Bennett?" I shocked myself with my gumption. Perhaps this was my head still in the clouds. But whatever happened to us being partners? This tone in Bennett's voice had been gone for quite a while, and I didn't want it returning. But instead of being the submissive little boy, I called him on it this time. I don't know why.

But it was his reply that shocked me even more. "Sorry, Andrew, I just want the best for you, that's all, I shouldn't have been so harsh."

And the air was cleared; then Bennett joined me on my run today, and we talked about everything from track to the summer to my future to Jennifer–that might have been a little too personal, but it didn't bother me any.

5/24/02

Shit.

We haven't had a day like this in months. About eighty degrees, sunny, warm. Yeah, Bennett cancelled practice today, as I expected, and I knew I had only one place to go: the beach. Fundamentally, this is not a problem; logistically it could be. In years past, this would be a beach volleyball day and I'd be there with the 'old' boys. But I obviously wasn't friends with them anymore.

Walking home from school, I contemplated going by myself, calling Jennifer, or seeing what Forrest was up to. I settled on the latter. I figured he'd have a friend or two and I really wanted to play some volleyball. Really, I just wanted to pound Darrin into the sand.

But I didn't have to call. On our answering machine was Forrest's message detailing his plan to be at the beach by three and to meet him there. Within minutes, I was out the door again and on my way. New England's long winters and wet springs always drained me; the first truly summer-like day was like winning the lottery.

Karma is a good thing, when it works for me, at least. At 2:54, I pretty much had the beach to myself. At 2:58, Darrin and his clan popped out of his car; simultaneously, Forrest and his posse (of two) hopped out of his car. I could literally feel the tension and see the whole scenario moving before me in super slow motion. Darrin and Chris were pointing at me laughing. Their two cronies who I'd never hung out with were joining in too. Clearly, Harris and I had been replaced in the foursome.

"He still thinks he's playing," Darrin chortled.

"There he is," Forrest rapped pointing at me.

And as I felt Darrin and Chris strutting over to insult me, they were cut off by Forrest walking over to hug me. Forrest quickly introduced me to two of his school friends, Jimmy and Dane. In the background, I could see Darrin and friends u-turning back to where they came from.

Right now, this sounds like the makings for an after school special gone terribly wrong. But it really isn't. We had a ball. Darrin had a ball. They had four; we had four. Just like trillions of times before, it was time to play, only this time I was on the other side of the net.

And it is always on this day that reality smacks me in the face. The first warm day serves as a shocking reminder to just how pale I am. Though most of May and April had hovered with temperatures in the 50's and 60 with limited sunshine, it doesn't change the fact that my arms and legs were exposed while my chest and back were covered. I could've blinded somebody when I took off my shirt. But no worries, I clearly wasn't the only one; all over the net resembled melting snowmen; at least I had a six pack of abs.

I love playing beach volleyball. And this time it was personal. I'd never played with Forrest, Jimmy, or Dane before, but we all understood the basics of the game. Most of the time I concentrated on playing and nothing else, but when the score was settled and we had won, I wanted to cry. And it wasn't the normal sickening cry that I feel when I was 'depressed,' but a cry of joy and vindication, that for some reason, I was better than all of them.

I remember that when I used to play on the other side of the net, win or lose, we always slapped five with the opposition at the end of the match. I decided that I would initiate it this time. True, my teammates didn't know the opposition, but they knew the history, much the same on the other side of the net. So when I approached the net and went to walk under, I nearly froze, would they meet me?

I think out of fear and having nothing against my teammates, they did. And Darrin came first. He said nothing, to me at least, but he did slap my hand, as did his teammates, who all said the obligatory good game, as did I, but I also said it to Darrin.

By six o'clock, I was left with the decision that had plagued me my whole life: responsibility. I knew that I should go home, eat, shower, read, relax, and sleep in preparation for tomorrow's meet, but I desperately wanted to hang out and spend the night with my new friends. Yet, for some reason, in my heart I knew that I owed Bennett this race. I'd come too far to just not care about States. I told my new 'boys' that it was time I crashed. They understood and wished me good luck.

I popped in my front door and saw Mom in the kitchen. She was cooking, which was weird on a Friday, but she was making pasta and chicken.

"What's up Mom?" I inquired.

"I figured I'd make something good for you tonight, you got a big race tomorrow."

How cool, I thought to myself, Mom was making a quality meal before my race, obviously it meant a lot to her too. For once in my life, I was proud of myself.

5/25/02

Not that running at State's wasn't a big deal, but it just seemed anticlimactic. I had dedicated my entire season to the goal of qualifying for State's, and I had. Cliche, true, but I was just happy to be here. Before the gun even went off, I was already thinking about how my goal for next season must be oriented around where I would place at State's, not just qualifying.

And the race was nothing to write home about. I finished ninth, ran a 9:56–yep, same time again. And walked off the track. Funny thing, though, crossing the finish line I wasn't collapsing as I was last time. Theoretically, that meant my body was better conditioned than last week, therefore also meaning that I didn't run as hard. But it wasn't physical effort that held me back, it was emotional and mental. I think Sanderson had the same problem, he finished tenth in 9:59. I couldn't stick with the lead pack at all and the next tier seemed just out of my reach for the whole race. In essence, I ran by myself–not close enough to catch anybody, nobody close enough to catch me.

At the end of the day, I was the ninth best runner in the entire state, and that is pretty cool.

"Today was a new beginning," I told Bennett after the race. "Now, I will begin working to be the best runner in the entire state."

"Go home, wash your uniform, and bring it back to me on Monday, then we'll talk about next year," Bennett's replied.

Fair enough.

Perhaps the biggest shock of the day, however, occurred when I opened my front door after the race. Mark was there. I had become so preoccupied with track and my own life, that I entirely forgot that he was coming home. Originally, I thought he'd be around for my race, but he chose to stay a couple extra days at school, leave most of his things in storage, and hop a ride home with a friend driving through to Boston.

I pledged to myself that I would make a concerted effort to be more brotherly towards him and not be so judgmental and edgy. In order to accomplish this, I knew two things must occur. First, I must extend an invitation to hang out with him. Second, I mustn't allow his snippy comments to unearth who I am as a person. Turn the other cheek. Ignore him. You know, all the cliches once again. But I'm willing to try.

So I greeted him with a "what's up brother" and a man hug.

He told me I smelt like shit.

So I laughed a bit, said I'd just finished top ten in the state, and then I hit the shower. So far, so good (another cliche–now I see why Blackwell yells at us for using them in our writing, they suck, they're so banal).

May 28, 2002

Walking to the locker room after school was a surreal experience. I'd come here everyday since the beginning of school, but today felt so different for so many reasons. For once, I wasn't going to run. And certainly turning in my uniform was a culmination of many ups and downs. From my 'grade' problem during cross country season, mediocre indoor season, and stellar outdoor season, tempered with my on again, off again relationship with Jennifer, Harris's death, a new peer group, and now a job; life had changed drastically. And yet, as I opened the door to the locker room, I had an eerie sensation that this wasn't an end point, but merely a point of many along the way, I just wasn't sure where I was going.

Since most of the team didn't qualify for State's, uniform collection was essentially over. In fact, as I walked in, Bennett was the locker room's only tenant.

"You got a minute," Bennett began.

"Sure, I'm not sure what to do with myself since I don't have practice today."

"For starters, I want you take ten days off to heal. Just relax and not worry about running. Hell, eat whatever you want."

"I kind of do still, my diet needs to improve. I did cut out fast food though."

Bennett smiled, perhaps amused that though I had come a long way as far as track discipline was concerned, he had a faint discovery that many other disciplines still needed to be mastered before I became a superstar. "We'll work on diet soon enough. There's something else I want to talk to you about, Andrew."

"Sure, what coach?"

"Well, over the weekend I spent a lot of time thinking about your season, and how far you've come in so many ways–personally, physically, academically, the whole deal. And I've heard you say that distance running truly is your passion."

"Yeah, I wish we had the 5000 at every track meet. In fact, I really look forward to the long distance days. I get to be me."

"I know, and during our run last week I heard you mention a bit about seeing the world and the experiences you want to have."

I was shocked that Bennett had remembered that. "You know coach, I talk to Mr. Blackwell a lot about that. Sometimes he encourages me to see the world like that, but at others he throws me a lot of stop signs and dirty looks."

"Well here's the deal, Andrew. Every year I run several marathons, mostly I go by myself. This summer I'm running a race in San Francisco and am spending two weeks traveling prior to the race. I wanted to talk to you about running the race and traveling the country."

I didn't know how to react, a small part of me feared that this was a freeze frame for an after school special regarding how to avoid being taken advantage of–after all I was alone in the locker room with my coach. But that thought quickly became laughable as I thought about who Bennett was. Another part of me was excited and relished the mere thought of traveling out to San Francisco and running the race. Part of me thought my parents would never go for this. And part of me was unsure about spending two weeks with Bennett. "Tell me more," a very safe response.

"Here's the deal. I'm taking the train across country to Seattle, renting a car, and exploring the Pacific Northwest and California. Then, after the race I'm flying back. The train is taken care of. I have a sleeping room and it has two beds. I also have my plane ticket already, you'd have to buy one too. As far as the race, you'd half to run the half marathon since you're too young to run the full marathon, you need to be 18 for that. Along the way I plan on going to some National Parks and staying at hotels along the way. Obviously we'd get two beds in the rooms."

I might add here that this last statement calmed me a lot.

Bennet continued, "We'd have to work out paying for a rental car and hotels plus food and other things, but I put together the whole trip in a folder for you if you're interested. I know you'd have to talk to your parents and I'd want to talk to them also to make sure everybody's on the same page."

I knew I needed time to think about this. Obviously I would love to see the country by train. And the thought of seeing so much of the country I'd never been to before was very alluring. The half marathon would certainly keep me training over the summer, and that too was a positive. But I didn't know how my parents would react plus the financial aspect of it. And there was definitely a part of me that didn't know if I was comfortable enough with Bennett to spend this much time with him.

"Coach, this sounds really cool. But I have to talk to my parents first and see what they say," a very safe response.

"Absolutely. And don't feel pressure to go or not to go. I figured if there was one person on the team who would appreciate this opportunity, it would be you. If it doesn't work out, I completely understand. And if it does, then we'll have quite a trip to look forward too. Do me a favor, think about it this week and let me know next week."

"Alright, thanks coach."

My premonition prior to entering the locker room seemingly had come true. Bennett's proposal had certainly offered a new point on the continuum that is my life. I was certainly intrigued by Bennett's proposal, I just didn't know where I stood yet.

Learning

May 28, 2002

After my meeting with Bennett, I walked home and found myself with nothing to do. I can't remember the last time I was home from school this early with nothing to do.

I picked up the folder Bennett had given me about going to San Francisco. I decided that if I wanted to go, I would mention it to Mom tonight, if I didn't want to go, I'd never bring it up at all. The first page in the folder was Bennett's itinerary, it included essentially two weeks of travel plans. The first three days were all on the train: New Haven to New York, change trains, New York overnight to Chicago, change trains, two nights Chicago to Seattle. I knew all about these trains, the Lakeshore Limited and Empire Builder would provide most of our service. According to Bennett's notes, he had reserved a room in each train, two beds, and meals. I must say, the lure of the train trip alone was fascinating. Seeing the country, traveling by train: two of my passions so delicately woven together.

Once in Seattle, we'd spend time in the city proper, plus Tacoma, Olympia, Astoria, Portland, then back to the coast through Oregon and Northern California, including Point Reyes, San Francisco, and even south to Monterey and Big Sur. Essentially, we'd travel 1 and 101 through Washington, Oregon, and California seeing the famed coast along the way. He'd listed the places of lodging for each city as well as planned places to go for each day; I must say it looked awesome, even though a good number of the places I'd never heard of. The trip culminated in the San Francisco Marathon and Half Marathon races. Bennett made it sound like that being too young for the marathon was a bad thing; I thought of it as more of a blessing. I couldn't imagine running a full marathon, the half alone was imposing enough.

I sat alone, pondering. The trip was awesome, but could I pay for it? Was I ok with going alone with Bennett? Yes.

At dinner, Mark bolted early to meet up with an old high school friend and Layne too left early for his guitar lesson. It left just Mom and me to finish dessert and clean up. I figured this would be the perfect opportunity to bring up Bennett's proposal.

While clearing some dishes, "Hey Mom, I want to talk to you about something."

"What is it?" neither maternally nor indifferently.

"Well Mr. Bennett wants me to run in a race this summer in San Francisco. And here's the deal, we'd be gone for two weeks and spend some time exploring the country."

"What?"

I must say, Mom's response didn't surprise me, in fact, it was very similar to my thoughts when Bennett first proposed the idea to me. "Yeah," I continued, "we'd take the train across country to Seattle, see the west coast, and eventually end up in San Francisco, where I'd run a half marathon."

"Do you want to go?" At this moment, I knew I had a chance.

"Yes. Bennett gave me a folder with a lot of information in it, I looked at it after school today and was wondering if you'd look at it tonight or tomorrow?"

"Bring me the folder Andrew, I'll look at it while you clean up the kitchen."

Nice move Mom, she just found away to make me do the counters, table, floor, dishes, trash, and leftovers, but I didn't mind given the circumstances. I think it took me twice as long as it should have to clean up, mostly because I was working quietly in anticipation of any reactions I might get from Mom. Plus, I moved slowly so she could fully digest the folder's contents.

Ironically, as soon as I finished the kitchen Mom was ready to talk once again. "Andrew," she began, "I think this would be great for you. But we need to sit down and figure out how much it's going to cost and how you're going to pay for it."

My insides were burning with ecstacy, but I didn't want to show that to Mom. However, I also realized just how much I wanted to go. "I know," I said, "that's what I was really worried about, paying for it."

"Well, you can work more hours now that practice is over. Except for Wednesdays when you have driver's education classes, the rest of your afternoons are free."

I had forgotten that driver's ed. started tomorrow, but I was keenly aware that I could pick up more hours at the grocery store. They'd been begging me to work weekdays, so hours wouldn't be a problem.

"I know," I partially lied, "I figured I could work Tuesday, Thursday, and Friday plus my normal Sunday shift. I was thinking too that once school let out I could work pretty much everyday and mow lawns too."

"Fifty fifty," Mom blurted out. "I pay half, you pay half. If you want to talk to your father and break it into thirds that's up to you."

"Deal." And I gave Mom probably the biggest hug I'd ever given anyone.

I sat in my room figuring how much the trip would cost as well as if I wanted to talk to Dad about it. I decided that I would tell him about what I was going to do, and if he offered to help out, so be it, if not, then it would be fifty fifty with Mom, which was fine by me.

"You can't go," Dad began.

"What, Mom said I could."

Less than an hour after Mom's approval, Dad was saying no. Strangely, he called the house on a Monday. Not really to talk to us, but more to inform us that a business trip was going to keep him out of town until really late on Friday and he wanted to switch weekends.

"You're not going to spend two weeks out west with some guy I don't even know, it's not right Andrew."

"You're some guy I don't even know," I said this to hurt him. "I see Bennett more hours in a week than I see you in a year. There's no way you're telling me whether or not I'm going. Mom can say no, not you."

"Andrew, I am your father and you will listen to me. The answer is no."

"Fuck you." I think this was the first time I cursed so blatantly to anyone. "You're like an uncle, not a father. My father would know what my homework was tonight. Do you? My father would know my friends. Do you? My father would see me more than a few hours a month. Do you? Fuck you Dad, I'm telling you I'm going."

"Put your mother on the phone boy."

"Don't call me boy."

"I'll call you what I want. Don't ever forget that I am your father and you are the boy."

"Fine. I'll call you what I want then. Asshole."

As I purposely dropped the phone on the floor prior to Mom picking it up, I could hear my father screaming something, but I couldn't make it out. I watched from just a foot or two away to see how Mom would handle this situation. Silent. That's what she was, I knew my father wasn't yelling at her–he always gave her that respect. But I knew he was 'putting his foot down' (sorry Blackwell).

"If Andrew wants to go, he can go. He's old enough to make that decision. I've talked to Mr. Bennett several times and he really watches out for Andrew."

A long pause.

"I would never put Andrew in a dangerous situation, and you know that."

A shorter pause.

"I told Andrew he and I would split it fifty fifty. If you want to contribute we'll go in thirds. And that's the end of it."

Mom handed the phone back to me.

"How much is this going to cost?" Dad inquired.

"It looks like around $2200 all said and done, including tickets, hotels, food, and spending money."

"I'll write a check to your mother for $1000 tonight. You two figure out the rest."

"Why?"

"Because you're going to go either way and I can't stop you. So at least I can make sure you get a few good meals and have enough money to get buy."

"Thanks Dad. Sorry about calling you an asshole." Actually, I wasn't, for some reason, I guess it helped to get my point across.

"You will be punished for that next weekend."

Understandable.

May 29, 2002

My first day of driver's education was not what I expected. I'm not really sure if I truly knew what to expect, but it wasn't this. I guess I pictured boring lessons about the gas pedal, rearview mirror, and traffic lights. Instead, our lesson began with a quiz regarding motor vehicle laws, anything ranging from speed laws, pedestrian laws, and alcohol laws. And this last topic served as the focal point of the lesson.

A PowerPoint presentation revealed information regarding blood alcohol content laws and statistics regarding alcohol related accidents, injuries, and fatalities. I obviously needed no reminder of the last category. But that's not what got me. It was the pictures.

The instructor kept interspersing pictures of mangled cars, deformed bodies, and distraught families. I held up ok during this part. But the video that came next was just too graphic. Bodies and tears everywhere. I felt sick, I wanted to leave, I wanted to cry, but I just sat there taking it. Harris.

I hadn't thought about him in a little while, which was a good and bad thing. Good because I was moving on and had coped with his death. Bad because I was beginning to forget him. And though I wasn't friends with the old crowd anymore, I still loved Harris. And class brought back too many painful memories.

At home, I told Mom about class and how it disturbed me. I think she understood, but she couldn't say anything that would make the sick, painful feeling inside of me go away. This feeling I had suppressed inside of me was returning with vengeance. I tried to think positively, about how I had promised myself that I wouldn't feel this way again. I yearned to focus on my goals, traveling out West, and making the most of everyday. But I couldn't. I just sat on the end of my bed, that sick feeling covering every vein in my body, overrunning the blood that flows through my arteries.

Several times I held the phone in my hand ready to call Jennifer. But I didn't. This was the Andrew that drove her away, the Andrew she loathed. The Andrew that I vowed to never be again. But she is my rock and understands me, so I dialed her number, but hung up before I could push the last digit. Alone, nobody to talk to, alone. She wouldn't want to see me like this. I promised Mom I'd tell her if I felt this way, but I didn't want to admit I was relapsing, so I said nothing, fearful that she'd make me see a doctor, or changer her mind about allowing me to go out west. So I said nothing, and sat on the end of my bed until I found it necessary to puke, which I did, and passed it off to Mom as a reaction to something I ate at school.

5/30/02

I contemplated staying home from school today, but I knew I had to go. I simply wouldn't allow myself to slip into self wallow. Mom asked me if my stomach felt better, for a second I hesitated, but then I remembered my lie regarding a tainted school lunch.

Before school started, I stopped by Blackwell's room and asked him if I could spend lunch with him today. It had been a while since we conversed outside of class, and I needed to talk to him, or at least spend lunch with him. I feared the sickly Andrew invading the lunch table, and thus repulsing Jennifer all over again. Also, I wanted a new book, I hadn't read anything since *Gatsby* and was ready for something new, anything I guess, to distract my mind.

"So what's going on, Andrew," Mr. Blackwell began, munching on a handful of peanuts. Nice lunch I thought to myself, but it was better than mine–I brought nothing.

"I had my first night of driver's ed. last night and it flipped me out. I thought I was over everything that happened with Harris, but watching the videos about drunk driving brought it all back a hundred times over. I couldn't sleep last night."

"You know, I'm not a shrink, but the last few weeks you've been so busy that you haven't had time to do anything except that which you had to do. I don't think you've read a book since *Gatsby*, which is unlike you."

"Actually, Mr. Blackwell, that's the other reason why I'm here, I want a new book."

Blackwell continued, "But it seems to me that you have spare time now that track is over and sitting in class last night triggered some painful memories that you haven't had time to think about in a while."

"I know, that's kind of what I figured too."

"You need not feel bad about remembering, but you do need to continue to do the things that make you happy. What does make you happy, Andrew?"

"Running, reading, hanging out with Jennifer, playing guitar, going to the beach."

"Which of those did you do after class last night?" Blackwell questioned while rummaging through a huge stack of books behind his desk that seemingly lost organizational structure years ago.

"None of them, I wanted to call Jennifer, but she hates this side of me, can you blame her?"

Emerging from his desk with a victorious look on his face, Blackwell concluded, "Well, here's a book, it's called *Catch-22*, it's long, it'll keep you busy, plus you'll like it. Now go eat lunch, with Jennifer, and be yourself, whoever that maybe."

Blackwell's last statement momentarily froze me, did he think I was crazy? Was I annoying him too? "Come again," I inquired.

"You need to decide who you want to be. I know, I know, you've said it to me before about traveling and living life to the fullest, but you can't say that's who you want to be, but then not be it."

"I know." And I did know, that's the worst part, I guess I just needed somebody to reinforce it to me.

Of course Jennifer wondered where I was the second I pounced down at the cafeteria with a cup of fries and an ice cream cone, and only a few minutes left to woof them down. Might I add, Bennett's proclamation that I could eat whatever I wanted for ten days and be as lazy as I wanted was paying off huge dividends.

"Hanging with Blackwell," I said through a mouthful of fries. I was giving it my best.

"Why?"

"Well," I pondered for a second, but passed it off as a gasp at my ice cream cone, "well, I wanted a new book to read and I wanted to ask him about going out west." This part was a lie, in fact, I hadn't even told him about my west coast plans for the summer, but I would immediately after class just in case Jennifer should inquire.

"What did he say?" she asked.

"He didn't say much about going out west, figure I'll talk to him about it after class, but he did give me *Catch-22* to read; he thinks I'll like it. Looks long, very long," I added.

"Oh, well, I was hoping you'd want to hangout this weekend, but I don't know if I can compete against *that* book," Jennifer flirtatiously replied.

"You've got the book beat, everyday," I so creatively responded.

And lunch ended up being just fine. In fact, after the initial awkwardness of the first moment, I walked away feeling just fine.

But that's also the problem. I don't want you to think that I can simply turn my emotions, feelings, and inner demons on and off. I can't. But I can do what Blackwell said. I can continue to do the things that make me happy. Then, I think about other things. But it's the idle time that captures me, and sends me down the path that I don't want to go down. And I fear that I will continually live my life in fear that those feelings will catch up with me. For now, though, I can find peace in the things and people that I enjoy. And today, that was enough.

5/31/02

As soon as school was over, I decided to call the grocery store to let them know I could work more hours. I was obviously going to need the money if going out west this summer was going to become a reality.

"Are you available now?" Margaret inquired.

"Yeah, I guess so."

"Good, both of my baggers called out tonight, you can work from whenever you get here until close."

And with that I was on my way for a seven hour shift. Luckily, the store was just a few minutes away by bike and the weather was cooperating. I left a note for Mom and was out the door.

Before I began my shift, Margaret asked about my new availability. I still hadn't figured Margaret out. Though she was the manager, I rarely saw her, especially since she only worked alternate Sundays and had called out sick on half of them. Margaret always seemed frazzled and overwhelmed, which was strange since she spent more time in the break room than any other employee in the store. Overweight and loud, she never stopped complaining about all that she had to do, yet, I rarely saw her doing much of anything. Long story short, I told her about working two weekdays, no Wednesdays, and whenever on the weekends.

"You can go to cashier training on Friday and Saturday next week," she blurted out, "once you finish your training, you'll work the register and get a raise. I need cashiers, by next Sunday you'll be a cashier."

"OK," was all I could reply with; it didn't seem I had much of a choice, I liked bagging, but more money was never much of a problem I guess.

My shifts with Forrest always seem to have extra flare. He was psyched to see me working a day other than Sundays, but bummed to learn that I'd be a cashier because that meant our fun and games with customers would have to end. So, we figured, we'd have to make the last couple of shifts winners. We'd grown tired of the games we had been playing with customers and decided it was time to come up with something new.

It was almost telepathic, we both knew what do. As some soccer mom with her two blonde haired trophies walked through the line, Forrest scanned a frozen pizza, saying to me, "Did you see that story about people dying from eating frozen pizza?"

"You mean from like bacteria from the pepperoni, right?" I replied.

"Yeah, apparently like ten kids died in Boston alone, kind of messed up. My mom threw away all of our frozen pizza."

"That's why I'm a vegetarian," I lied, "prevents me from eating poop that gets into the meat."

"WHAT!" screamed the lady, "do you know what brand it was? I don't want these now, take them back."

"OK," said Forrest, and he voided the order, the lady in a panic.

But we both knew that wasn't good enough. We had to do more. A little scare with frozen pizza was child's play, we needed a bigger score. And we both saw it coming.

While passing back a jar of tomato sauce, Forrest began, "Andrew, I still can't believe we're selling this stuff after that whole blood scare."

"I know, some lady in Florida got AIDS because there was blood in the sauce. She couldn't tell, you know, 'cuz it's red and all."

"That one dude claims he got herpes from it," Forrest took over, "he's got all types of sores all over his lips now. Looks like a freak show, puss oozing everywhere."

The customers, a pair of older, stuffy types, seemed not to notice at first, or maybe they were just ignoring our mindless banter. But sooner or later we knew that Mr. and Mrs Old Money returning from winter in Florida would perk up.

So I continued our game, "The hospitals are overrun because I guess if you got type A blood and the sauce got type B blood it can cause all types of reactions. Kind of wonder how all this blood got in the sauce."

"Apparently it was some sick joke. The factory workers were pissed about being screwed out of overtime so they tainted the sauce. You know, I guess they knew people wouldn't notice the red."

"Really," I inquired, a little lost where to go from here.

"Yeah," Forrest continued as if he'd be rehearsing this his entire life, "you name it, cuts, bloody noses, needles, it all goes in the sauce, and so many people are doing it that it's nearly impossible to trace it to who. Sometimes two or three people will bleed into the same jar."

"God, I'd hate to think what the milkman does to the milk," I interjected.

And then it happened, the Mrs. fainted, down to the ground, shocking her oblivious husband who seemed woozy himself. Withering on the floor, gasping for air while dry heaving, the lady tried to regain some sense of class and grounding.

And Forrest didn't miss a beat, he grabbed his register phone, and paged, "Manager to register six for customer assistance please." But even more impressive, however, was the fact that he read the total to the stunned gentleman while he was trying to upright his ailing wife. Forrest repeated, "One-o-eight-thirty six, sir. How would you like to pay?"

Still searching for a sense of reality, the man stopped everything, looked from his wife to Forrest, to his wallet, and froze. "What?"

"I said, sir, one-o-eight-thirty six, and I need to know how you're going to pay since I've got a long line."

By this time the woman was standing again and the frazzled man was digging into her pocketbook for money while she precariously steadied herself at the front of their carriage. I don't know what provoked me to say it, but I did, "Oh no, dude I'm bleeding, I think I cut myself bagging their order. I got blood on my hands and I can see some on the bags."

And down she went again. Forrest was convulsing trying to hide his excitement, the man was dumbfounded again, this time with bills floating through the air as he pathetically grabbed for his fallen spouse.

"Manager to register six for customer assistance, thank you," Forrest paged again for Margaret, who never bothered to show up the first time.

When Margaret finally arrived, to say the least there was a scene. Customers at the front of Forrest's line were concerned for the twice fallen former princess while customers at the end of the line grumbled about long lines that weren't budging.

After the paramedics left, we were both called into Margaret's office. "So what happened, the lady said you two were talking about blood?"

"Yeah," I immediately jumped in, trying not to look guilty, secretly laughing on the inside while trying to stop my armpits from dripping nervous sweat. "I told Forrest that I think I got a paper cut and I needed to go wash my hands. That customer wanted paper bags and I must have cut myself opening one. I didn't notice it until I was done with their order. But you know, I thought it would be inappropriate to be handling people's food while bleeding. So I told Forrest I was going to wash my hands."

"And then she just fainted. So I paged a manager for help."

"Her husband said she fainted twice and you two were talking about blood in the spaghetti sauce!" Margaret shouted, seemingly unconvinced of our concoction.

For a second we both sat silently. Finally I spoke up. "Yeah, I guess she did faint twice, she tried getting up, but fell back down."

"That was right when I told the husband that I was going to get him a new jar of sauce because I thought I saw a speck of Andrew's blood on the lid from the paper cut," Forrest continued the charade.

"Go back to work, knock off the games you two; I don't have the time to deal with this stuff; the store's packed, we're down a cashier and a bagger, I've got too much on my plate. I don't need you two adding to it." Typical overworked Margaret, too lazy to discipline us, too 'busy' to care too much. Forrest and I returned to work; Margaret took a break.

I phoned Mom just after ten telling her I was hanging out with Forrest and he'd bring my bike and me home. It's funny, a few months ago I had to beg Mom for permission to go anywhere, even when I wasn't grounded, but now, I simply told her where I was going and that was that. Tonight, I didn't even know where I was going, we had no plan, the beach closed in an hour, and neither one of us really had any friends to call. Forrest's two mates were at some show in the city, and well, I had no mates, except for Jennifer.

So I called her. And remarkably, Jennifer and her friend Amy, who I actually liked, were just watching television, doing nothing. Perfect, a pseudo double date and ten minutes later we landed in Jennifer's driveway. After the obligatory introductions, we were still stuck with the simple fact that we had no plan, and perhaps that was the best plan. We ditched my bike at Jennifer's in order to make room for everyone, and started driving, to where we weren't exactly sure, but I'm not sure that it mattered. After a pass through of downtown screaming out the lyrics of our favorite songs, or whichever song happened to be on the radio, we finally parked at the local all-night diner.

Though still relatively early, barely eleven, the stoners were already settled which meant the drunks wouldn't be far behind, but we ignored them and had our own little world. Though I mostly engaged in the trivial conversation ranging from the 'who do you know game' to favorite movies and songs, occasionally I just listened. And while I listened, I thought to myself how wonderful this moment was. And I was normal, with friends, just hanging out. I wanted to capture that moment forever, to put it in a box and be able to take it out whenever I wanted to, for I was just Andrew, hanging out with his friends, having a good time.

After cheese fries, mozzarella sticks, and chicken fingers, we continued our drive to nowhere, eventually settling in for the midnight movie downtown. Some Tommy Lee Jones movie that I'd never heard of, but it didn't matter; I think I fell asleep a couple of times, but never deeply for though I don't remember the images, I do remember the sounds. By the end of the movie, all four of us, exhausted, were leaning on each other, and it was strangely romantic.

The drive back to Jennifer's house was much quieter than the drive from her house, but the hour was approaching two and sheer exhaustion had set in. Back in her drive way, all four of us hopped out of the car under the pretense of grabbing my bike. But in the end we all hugged each other and promised to gather at the beach tomorrow afternoon. And though I knew in my heart that it was teenage chivalry and not a contract, it didn't bother me, for I knew that tonight was a huge step forward.

June 1, 2002

I was still plastered to my bed when Mark burst through the door to wake me. I'd forgotten all about the deal we made. Since he gained his freshman fifteen–I thought that was for girls, but anyways–he wanted to get himself back in shape for the summer. But come on, it was barely eight o'clock in the morning on Saturday, the only day I could sleep in since I have to go to early mass before work on Sundays.

But Mark was already in his new shoes, shorts, and t-shirt. So, I had no choice. I pried myself from bed and met him in the living room. He was doing some newfangled stretching routine that must keep chiropractors in business. Part of me wanted to laugh hysterically, the other part just wanted to sleep.

"Like this," I rasped still wiping sleepy sand from my eyes and I began to lead Mark through a quick, but thorough stretching routine.

"I don't want to spend the whole morning stretching Andrew, that's not going to get me into shape."

"If you pull a muscle on the first day, then you'll never be able to get into shape, this will only take ten minutes, plus you won't be so sore after running."

Mark seemed to find the logic in my argument, and actually agreed without any further commentary, in fact, he even asked what the purpose of some of the stretches were, and then wondered how I could hold them for so much longer than him.

"Flexibility," I answered, "when I first started running I couldn't touch my toes, now I can eat them. It'll come. So how far do you want to run today?"

I don't think time or distance had occurred to Mark yet, "I don't know, maybe do three miles on the first day."

"Ok, I know a couple of routes we could take, we'll pick one. I'm not supposed to start running again until Monday, but it's close enough, we'll just take it a bit easy."

"I don't want to take it easy on the first day Andrew; you can tell me where to go if you can't keep up."

I started to laugh aloud, I think Mark had momentarily forgotten that I was the ninth best two miler in the State, keeping up wouldn't be a problem. Nonetheless, I largely ignored his remark and indicated a choice of routes, one mainly on road, the other mostly trail that we could choose from. Mark chose the road course and we were on our way.

About a quarter mile into the run, Mark mumbled to slow down. "I thought we were going to take it easy on the first day," he questioned.

Truth was, though I intended to take it easy, I hit the course like a rocket, just wanted Mark to know for sure who was in charge here. But I wouldn't let him know that. And luckily my stamina was still very strong, so despite the blistering start, I was still fresh in the lungs, not breathing hard at all as I replied, "We are taking it easy, I'll slow things up a bit."

"Thanks," Mark huffed through painful gasps.

By the end of the first mile, Mark and I were no longer communicating, but I knew he was too stubborn to turn around and too proud to admit this was killing him. True, I had slowed the pace down to a crawl, but crawling to me was sprinting to him. Having not ran for a week, this moment felt great. The days off meant the healing that Bennett spoke of and nothing hurt; my body was a machine.

Making a right onto Lumberton and now heading for home with just over a mile to go, Mark panted, "Go ahead, I'll meet you back at the house."

I didn't need to be offered twice. With a simple nod of my head, I was off, not too fast, but with an added burst. I let my legs determine the pace: long, slow strides focusing on rhythm more so than speed. By the time I reached my house, my legs were ready for more, though my lungs had lost a step or two as I felt an extra need for air and tightness in my chest. I've always heard that the lungs go first, now I know why. Several minutes later, Mark waddled down the driveway in obvious exhaustion. I tossed him a bottle of water which he held onto for dear life with one hand as he used his other hand to steady himself on the rail leading up to our house.

After a quick shower, we found ourselves gathering breakfast from the kitchen. I used this meal as my gateway back into healthy eating. Though I enjoyed my week of gluttony, my insides were definitely ready to get back to normal. "Brother," Mark began, "I don't know how you do it."

"What?" I asked, with intended naivety.

"You weren't even trying and I couldn't keep up with you at all. I never realized how hard it is to run like you do."

And I knew at that moment that Mark had a new found respect for how I spent my time after school and on weekends. Watching from the stands during an indoor meet several months back, I remember Mark shaking his head in disapproval as I fell apart in the two mile. Yet now he knew what it was like to run, and that clearly made all of the difference. I decided to be the good brother, "No worries, you'll see that everyday gets a little easier. The first two weeks will really suck. But once you clear that, the rest is pretty easy. The body gets stronger, and it's a great feeling. But most people quit after a day or two. Give it at least two or three weeks, then decide from there."

"Thanks."

"Tell you what Mark, go running everyday while I'm at school. Then once school gets out we'll run together. You can help me train for San Francisco and I'll help you get in shape. But it won't work unless you got a bit of a base, so you got like three weeks to get into shape."

"Deal," Mark contracted and for the first time in a while, I actually liked my brother, so much so that when Forrest careened into my driveway ten minutes later to make good on our beach day, that I actually asked Mark to come. Though he declined sighting other plans, it was a genuine offer, and Mark knew that.

June 3, 2002

As promised, Bennett was hanging around after school, and it was a welcome sight because I wanted to tell him the good news about me being in for the west coast trip. He was pretty nonchalant about the whole deal. But I guess he had to be. I think Bennett knew all along that I would be in; he came prepared with another copy of the itinerary, travel expenses, and miscellaneous details.

I had a lot of work to do–both running and at the grocery store.

I don't remember the last time that I felt this good, and I'm not sure why I do today, but I do. And I don't want to say anything else, except that I feel good.

June 6, 2002

The sun rises on Long Island Sound, but sets on the East River. I've learned to time runs so that in the morning I coast along the Sound and in the evening along the River. During the school year, this means weekends across public beaches and small commercial strips, and during the week nights past houses on stilts occupied only during the summer. With the passing of Memorial Day, the average age of my town has skyrocketed. Something seems strange about beautiful raised houses with Cadillacs in the sandways. Dune buggies seem more appropriate, but either way, the houses and views are still beautiful. It's my fourth day running past the same sun worshipers, and now they're used to me. Shirtless, bleached blonde hair flopping in multiple directions, and shorts too short for a boy to really be wearing, I must look like the poster child of what to avoid plastered to every wall of the senior center. At first, they just backed away from me; it appeared several ladies even reached for their cell phones just in case–but I just kept on running. Now, they wave at me, with bleached smiles and fashion jewelry way too elegant for a day at the beach.

I try to run as the sun is setting while the sun is making its daily escape, coloring the sky with new hues everyday, while the imported locals munch on dessert, sipping on mixed drinks. I try to catch the horizon, though its over the water, I can see the darkness behind me and the light in front of me. And towards the water, the sun sets, creating a finite horizon that seems graspable, but I know I can't run to it, so instead I run with it. On the shore, I lose myself in thought and see my future spread out in front of me, but so much of it must wait for time. I can't catch it now, but I'll never stop running for it; just like the horizon, far away now, but everyday I run just one step closer to it.

This time of the year is perfect too. Warm June days still have beautiful, breezy evenings. Unlike July and August when even at sunset, the air stifles the lungs, sea breezes disappear, and humidity chokes the lungs.

Since I have to be at work by four, I hit the beach just before three. It's hot. The first true summer day this year. Weatherman said low 90's and I'm feeling every one of those degrees. Wrinkled feet tiptoeing in the still cool waters–the water will need another two or three weeks to reach bathing temperatures–stepped back to watch me run along the blistering sand. Along the beach, I've learned how to quickly discard my shoes, leave them, run, loop back, and relace them without my heart rate dropping. Today, I regretted it. I could feel the sand burning my feet, despite my speed.

So I did it. Full speed, in front of the old ladies and gents, full speed, above my head until I couldn't run anymore, I sprinted into the water. Though my balance initially suffered, I quickly regained it and continued my jaunt along the sandbar several yards out until the water dipped again. Until it became too deep, then I started to swim, nearly reaching the other side of the river, then I turned back, and swam back to shore. My lungs were exploding–I'm a terrible swimmer, and the combination of brackish waters and sweat were stinging my eyes. But none of that mattered, the beach club was cheering my return to land and my second wind kicked in.

On my way to work today, I noticed that my body was sunburnt.

June 7, 2002

I haven't been this nervous in a long time, but I have good reason, or so I think at least. Jennifer and I are going on a date. Just the two of us. Though we've hung out quite a bit lately, it's always with other people or under the clear understanding that we're just friends. But not tonight, I made that point clear at lunch today. In my normal awkward way, I stumbled over words trying to surmise Jennifer's evening plans. When none existed, that's when the stuttering and spitting truly began. Eventually, I gurgled a decipherable message about us going on a date. Jennifer was cool with it, but she reminded me that dates and boyfriends were two different things. Immediately I agreed, but I hope there's room for discussion on that topic tonight; I'm not sure where she stands.

I have no idea what we should do, the typical movie seems too mundane and won't afford the conversation time I desire. I want to pick something really cool and memorable without being cheesy. So, as always, I turn to Mom. Weary and tired after work, Mom doesn't seem overly excited about my date, but I know if I nag her enough she'll eventually suggest something, even if it's just to shut me up.

"Take her to the beach, have a picnic, watch the sunset. Girls love that type of stuff," Mom hollers from the kitchen while I shave my peach fuzz in the bathroom.

"What type of food?" I inquire.

"I don't know, so long as I don't have to make it. You work at a grocery store, pick something out."

And that's exactly what I do. Noting that it's closing in on 5:00 already and Jennifer's parents will drop her off at 6:00, I grab my bike and race to the store all the while picturing in my mind what I'm to buy. We could make dinner and take it to the beach, and that would be cool too, there's that talk time I want. Similarly, I could buy ingredients for sandwiches and we could make a quick meal, or, the stand-by deli counter meal. I cover the distance to the store in just over five minutes and throw my bike around a light pole chaining it securely.

Once inside the store, practicality takes over and I realize that not only must I bike the food home, but I also must be able to transport the final product to the beach. Cooking is out. Deli counter is in.

Luckily my grocery store is always busy and perpetually understaffed–the number being served is 209, I'm 226. Time is of an essence in two entirely different ways: I need time to decide what I want; I need to hurry home and shower before Jennifer arrives. Anyways, as I wait my turn, I peruse the salads, wraps, and sides. Balancing taste, price, and transportability, I decide on artichoke salad, pasta salad, and turkey wraps. Judging by the nonchalance of the customers and workers, I sprint towards produce and grab a pint of strawberries and a tray of shortcakes. Checking back at the deli, number 220 is being served and I race towards dairy for whipped cream. Lightning must've struck as I hear my number being called as I jog back towards the deli, luckily Evelyn recognizes me and tells me to slow down, there's no rush. I'm sure the scores of people in line disagree, but I don't slow down and I spew my order to Evelyn quickly.

We're taught to be friendly at work, a concept I largely ignore when I'm working with Forrest, but it seems the employees with the highest rankings and the most awards are the friendliest. I have no awards and a remarkably mediocre ranking. Evelyn is number one in the deli and number two store wide. Perhaps it's the friendly small talk and the nostalgic stories about the food people order. Either way, I'm in a rush and could give two shits that she made the artichoke salad and it's tangy, sweet, delicious. I want her to scoop my food, tag it, and show some alacrity.

I circumvent Evelyn's cheerfulness by explaining my running–you know, the whole time frame thing, and this seems to light a flame under Evelyn. Though she continues to talk, she's now scooping too and the process is underway.

By the time I pay and carefully bike home, much slower this time so as to prevent a spill, it's approaching 5:45 and I fly through the shower dousing my body in liquid cleanser, dry, and litter myself with body spray. The name of the spray catches my eye, "Goodnight," and I think to myself how this could be a good night, in so many ways.

Jennifer wears jean shorts with a spaghetti strap tank top that highlights her petit frame perfectly. I notice the tan of her skin juxtaposed to the blonde streaking through her hair. Girls coordinate so much better than guys. I'm wearing khaki shorts and a blue polo, my standard hanging out in summer outfit. I don't know what part of me it compliments, probably none.

Jennifer helps me repack the meal into a more convenient carrying case and we raid Mom's kitchen for drinks, utensils, and napkins. Before leaving, I grab my guitar and hoist it on my back. Tucked inside a pocket is my digital camera and Jennifer carries a beach blanket that Mom produces from the trunk of her car; I'm worried about its cleanliness, but I don't say anything.

The beach curves in many directions, but we want to see the sunset, so we face west and pick a spot where sand meets rock. I wasn't the only genius with the beach picnic idea as numerous couples and families span the area.

By the time we set up and get comfortable, the sun is already beginning its nightly descent, but we have plenty of time to watch it drop so effortlessly towards a drifting horizon always just beyond my grasp.

Dinner conversation is largely small talk surrounding the food, beach, school, and my trip this summer with Bennett. It's not the conversation that I want, but it's too early in the evening to breach the relationship subject.

After the meal, I instinctively reach for my guitar and strum "Staring at the Sun" by U2. Jennifer immediately recognizes it and tells me to sing it, just don't play it. I stop playing immediately and make her promise not to laugh, she agrees, and I start again.

Initially I play and sing softly, almost to myself. Scared of embarrassing myself or disturbing our neighbors, I wait for her reaction.

"Louder," she whispers to me.

And when the chorus comes again, I play with more confidence and sing louder. Jennifer is smiling and I don't want the song to end, so as I approach the last line, I launch directly into "Gone til November," by Wyclef Jean, a song I can easily strum, but have no chance of singing well. But I go for it anyway and Jennifer doesn't laugh.

By now, the sun is speeding his way through the sky and starting to light the dusk with oranges, reds, and deep purples. I pull my camera out and snap several images of the sky, but I know I need Jennifer in them to make the pictures truly beautiful.

I grab her hand and lead her to the water, which is starting to warm a bit, but early June is still chilly for swimming, so we stand ankle deep and gaze into the distance. An older couple with a dog pass behind us and I implore them to take our picture. A moment I've been waiting for, but I'm scared to death. Initially, I want to lift Jennifer into my arms like a groom on his wedding day, but I decide against it, and I also decide against kissing. So I wrap my arm around her and she does the same to me and our picture is beautiful in so many ways.

Once the sun falls of the edge, there's only a little bit of time before complete darkness sets in and I don't like walking the narrow roads home on sightless nights. We pack our things and start for my house. Along the way I mention star gazing, but Jennifer's never done it, so the next phase of our date will involve blankets and my backyard–a perfect time for our conversation, I clandestinely think to myself as we race darkness.

By the time we empty our belongings at my house and have a suitable amount of small talk with Mom, the stars are dancing amongst themselves and Jennifer and I head for the backyard. Dew is already forming on the grass and the air has a hint of a chill, but not enough to use an excuse to keep somebody else warm.

We silently stare at the sky until I break the stillness pointing out the Dippers and Orion's belt.

Jennifer whispers, "How do you know all of this?"

"I love everything that has to do with nature and the weather. I read a lot about it and watch way too much Weather Channel."

"You watch the Weather Channel," Jennifer chuckles, "so does my dad. I think he has it on loop on our desktop."

"Do you ever wonder about the universe?"

"What do you mean?"

I want to sound philosophical, romantic, and profound without sounding arrogant, "Like how big the universe is, how far away the stars are, and how small we are in the whole scheme of things?"

Jennifer pauses before answering, "No."

"I think about it a lot," I begin, knowing where I'll end and fearing every second of it. "I sit out on the porch at night and just watch the stars, moon, or sometimes the lightning. During the day I do the same thing with the sun and water. I just think, about things, mostly about life and how we all came to be. I wonder if there's a God who cares about me or if it's just a human rationalization. I wonder how life began and how that star came to be. I wonder where I'm going in life and where I'll be in five or ten years and who will be there with me. And the only answer I come up with is that I want you to be there with me." And it's out. I'm sure she saw it coming and mostly ignored my ramblings about life and nature, which did come from the heart, but were certainly serving as catalysts for my main motivation.

The moment between me finishing and Jennifer responding felt endless, though I'm sure it was closer to immediate. "Only time will tell Andrew," was her response.

Then she changed the subject to which star is that one, and though I didn't know where I'd be years from now, I had just discovered that Jennifer wouldn't be there with me.

June 9, 2002

Though I still don't enjoy it, I'm learning to have fun while working the register. Usually Forrest and I convince the manager to assign us to registers right next to each other. This allows us to continue some of our childish games, though to a much more mundane level, especially since Margaret was on to us–she would never allow us to pair up like this, but she rarely works Sundays and today is no different.

Produce has codes. I type the code, the register does the weighing and the price magically appears. I type 4011 and bananas appear for 52 cents a pound. I've learned though. Watermelon is heavy, but cheap by the pound. Basil is light, but expensive by the pound.

I see my victim, a person who comes through my line it seems like every shift. And he's such a prick. One day he argued over buy one get one free, claiming since he only wanted one he should get it for half price. I thought he was kidding, so I laughed, which sent him into quite a tizzy. Luckily Margaret knew him and told me not to worry about it. I think he stormed out refusing to ever shop here again.

But he's back with a cartload of groceries and I see both basil and watermelon. I purposely grab both while he's still unloading the carriage and unable to see the screen. On the scale, I type the basil code for watermelon, suddenly his three dollar melon is over twenty dollars. For the basil, I know I can't use the watermelon code so I place it on the scale and find that some strange mushroom we sell is quadruple that of basil, so I type that for the basil and he's paying close to sixteen dollars for less than four dollars worth of basil. I fly through his order today, smiling and being friendly all the while. When I total him up, he seems shocked–I leaned on the scale a couple of times too for good measure on things like apples, pears, and peaches to hike up the price a little. He asks me to read back his receipt, which I do, including watermelon and basil.

"Can you give me the prices?" he summons.

"I can give you the receipt once the order is completed so you can go through it, but I can't do that now with such a long line."

Confused, and still taken by my unusual friendliness, he acquiesces and pays a fortune for his groceries.

"Look at him," Forrest points at my victim, who is contorting his body in all types of shapes at the customer service desk.

"I'll tell you later," I say, not wanting to inform him of my trick with customers in front of me.

But Forrest isn't ready to let this one go and my register phone rings. "Talk quietly, Andrew, tell me what you did to him," Forrest begs.

I whisper, "I screwed up his produce by typing wrong codes and leaning on the scale, I must have charged him an extra fifty bucks."

Forgetting the whispering game, Forrest hangs up the phone and turns to face me from his register, "That's fucking genius, asshole," so that everyone in both of our lines stare at him.

"Yeah, I try."

By now Charlene is striding my way with the customer. I think I'm screwed, but remarkably Fortune finds me in her providence today.

"Andrew," Charlene begins, "I think something's wrong with your scale. All of this gentleman's produce is much more than it should be."

"Really," I feign caring. "Let me check this customer's order."

As I carefully check her estimated weights against my actual scale weights, I remarkably find that the scale is fine. I suggest to Charlene and the customer, "Did you leave anything right by the register, like a purse, that could've affected the scale?"

"I don't carry a fucking purse you idiot!"

And my mission's accomplished, I've ticked him off once and for all, but before I can reply he continues, "Plus this asshole charged me for mushrooms instead of basil."

"First of all, you didn't have mushrooms. Secondly–

"I know asshole, you charged them to me!"

"–secondly, you are never allowed in my line again. I'm working my ass off for barely minimum wage and I certainly don't get paid enough to be insulted by pricks like you."

Charlene tries to intervene, "Andrew, let's fix his order now and then we'll agree that he'll use a different register in the future."

Knowing that I have the power, especially since two cashiers called in sick and the lines are seven and eight deep, I persist, "Charlene, I will not serve this man. I know you wouldn't let him talk to you that way. I've watched you kick customers out for saying far less. You have two choices, walk him away from me now and take care of it yourself, or I'm walking out the door right now."

Charlene cringes while freezing, I continue with the next customer. I glance at the man and Charlene standing there, I turn with a box of frozen peas in my hand, "I'm serious, he leaves now, or I leave now."

They both stand there, as do I, partially scared that I just might've gone too far and could force myself to walk out of a job I desperately need. And just as I lower the peas, and turn towards the exit, Charlene stops me, "Ok, I'll take care of it, you stay and ring up the customers."

"Asshole, you fucking asshole," the man lands one last jab.

My phone rings immediately, Forrest. "I need your balls."

"I learned it by watching you," I do my best Don't Do Drugs Commercial.

At break time, I know Charlene will let me have it, so instead I let her have it. Luckily she's a college kid home from break who's not really a manager, but a shift supervisor.

"How dare you let that guy call me every name in the book and just stand there. You never let anyone talk that way about you or anyone else and you let him berate me."

"Andrew," Charlene begins.

But I won't let her, "NO! I'm not done. I rang up his whole order correctly, I don't know what he's talking about mushrooms for, he didn't even buy any. I don't get paid nearly enough money to get talked to like that. I can't believe you just stood there. I have half a mind to report that to Margaret; she never would allow that."

"Andrew," Charlene begins again. "At first I thought you and Forrest were playing one of your games. But then I realized you weren't. I'm sorry. And the mushrooms, well it's one digit off from watermelon so I think you hit a wrong code on that one. Probably an accident."

"Probably," I pounce on her, not yet ready to accept her apology, "definitely, I don't even know the mushroom code. But I know watermelon. I must've mishit the keypad."

"Yes," Charlene replies, "Again, I'm sorry and I don't think Margaret needs to know about this."

"Fine, but not again," I conclude.

I love my job.

June 13, 2002

I finished Blackwell's exam in record time. Partially because I knew the material cold, partly because it was my last exam and summer vacation was set to begin.

Sitting at my desk awaiting my classmates to finish and the dismissal bell to ring, I knew I wanted to say something to Blackwell before leaving, but I wasn't sure what. He was my friend, teacher, mentor, and in some ways, nemesis. Not because he was evil or fought against me, but because he was willing to ground me. Not like a parent grounds a child, but he put me in my place and forced me to think logically. Though Blackwell never directly dashed any of my dreams, he always reminded me that a dream was nothing without implementation, which was the hardest part. I needed that in my life. Someone to help me put things in perspective, especially since Mom was too busy to and Dad wasn't there to.

I intentionally waited for the class to empty, which didn't take but a second seeing how it was the last day, then I strolled towards Blackwell's desk. "I wanted to say thank you for, you know, everything you did for me this year. So, ummm, thanks." I amaze myself with my eloquence from time to time.

Blackwell's response seemed scripted, "You're a good kid Andrew. You have tons of potential and one of my jobs as a teacher is to make sure that my students are utilizing their abilities and making something of themselves."

"Well, thanks again. You think it'd be cool if I emailed you after the whole west coast trip and let you know how it went?"

"I'd like that," Blackwell replied, "how about before you go we grab a bite for lunch and we'll discuss *Catch-22*. You still owe me a book, you know."

"Truth is, I haven't started yet. But I will, now that school's out I'll have some time and will do that. We don't leave for like a month or something, so I'll make sure I'm done with it before we meet for lunch."

"Deal."

And that was that, it wasn't the farewell I imagined, but I also knew that it wasn't farewell, and I'm really happy about that.

Normally I look forward to summer vacation with tremendous anticipation, and to a degree, I am once again. But I know this year will be much different. Showing up at the beach and knowing my crew will be there is a thing of the past. True, I will still play some volleyball with Forrest and his friends, but I know it won't be as often and it will have to be scheduled. Part of me wishes that I possessed the courage to simply hang out at the beach and join a team looking for a fourth, but I'm too self-conscious to do that, and I know it.

Leaving Blackwell's room, I felt a quiet peace or tranquil anticipation, if that makes any sense whatsoever. The west coast is my main focus, though traveling with Bennett does make me a bit nervous still, I just hope it's not weird. Plus training for the San Francisco race will provide me something to focus on everyday. The grocery store will occupy quite a few hours and there's some places I want to see in New Haven and New London, maybe Jennifer will come with me, but we haven't spoken since our night beneath the stars. A dream is nothing if it's not worked towards, so I can't worry about who will or will not be going with me, I must keep moving forward.

So this summer I will tour Yale University, visit Ocean Beach, see Mystic Seaport, and take a day trip to Block Island, among other things.

June 15, 2002

A car crashed through Mom's garage today, completely destroying the garage door, denting the Nissan's bumper, cracking a headlight, and bruising my ego: I was the driver of the car that crashed through Mom's garage today.

Now that drivers' education is winding down, I needed more practice on the roads before Mom would even dream of actually letting me get my license. I never made it to the road today. Though I did learn that the red 'R' stands for reverse while the green 'D' stands for drive.

As I looked behind me to back out of the driveway, I took my foot off the brake and punched the gas peddle. The car, to my astonishment, rocketed forward, almost immediately into the garage. Mom screamed horrifically, pulling the emergency brake while I engaged the anti-lock brakes. But it was too late; the damage was done.

Mom never checked to see if I was alright, but I think she assumed so given that we really weren't traveling that fast, plus she was just fine. But she did call me a lot of names, all of which were derogatory. By the end of her tirade, I knew that I was an idiot and that I had better pick up more hours at the grocery store. Despite it all, I managed to take a few photos because rarely do you see a car through a garage door; it did look pretty funny. Mom didn't think so.

A few hours ago, Mom burst into my room crooning, "Andrew, did you save the pictures you took of the car in the garage?"

"Yes, why?"

"Because I called the insurance company and it looks like they'll cover the garage and the car with only a fifty dollar deductible. Boy are you lucky."

And she was right, I was very lucky, this was only going to cost me fifty dollars, instead of the hundreds I was anticipating. Not satisfied, though, I replied, "No Mom, smart. Everybody makes mistakes–I made one today..."

"A big one and a stupid one," Mom interjected.

"Hey, you were the one who got confused and ripped out the oil pan on the sidewalk last year, I mean who drives on a sidewalk, but people make mistakes mother! So anyway, as I was saying, smart, I made a mistake, but was smart enough to photograph it for the insurance company, even though somebody was screaming at me and calling me names. Did I call you names after you planted the car on the sidewalk, ripping out the oil pan?"

"Oh shut-up Andrew, just get me the pictures and that'll end it."

And that did end it, in fact, Mom even said she'd pay the fifty bucks herself, maybe she did feel bad for all that name calling earlier, or maybe she just didn't want me to open my mouth again.

June 19, 2002

It's amazing how summer is now just a week old, but the routine is clearly established. Every weekday, including Friday, I work at the grocery store from four until close, which is ten. Ironically, Forrest has the same hours. Part of me can't believe that Margaret would let us work together everyday, especially considering how much she hates both of us, but the other part of me think that Margaret does this to spite both of us. Nobody in their right mind wants these shifts. After eight, only two cashiers work, so why not put us both on with a manager, apparently she thinks we can be tamed that way. But it doesn't matter, it plays into both of our hands.

Mornings mean sleep, I usually pry myself out of bed by ten so I can go running and fulfill the list of chores Mom leaves for me. Usually it's something simple, like trash and dishes. Except yesterday I had to trim the hedges, that took a bit longer, but was kind of fun too. By noon Forrest is in my driveway and we're on our way to the beach. It's funny, I was worried about not having a crew, but when you start with two, it becomes easier to make friends. Forrest's friends both work at a golf course, so they can't play. We're always looking for two more. And after just a few days of this charade, people are now approaching us; I guess our nearly perfect record on the court speaks for itself. I see the old crew down there a lot too. We've played a few games against them and won most of them. But the awkwardness is gone and so are the pleasantries and animosities. They're just strangers who I play volleyball against, like the countless other foursomes that'll play on the other side of the net this summer and in years gone by. None of our new partners have become friends, yet. But I'm fine with that.

By three we leave the courts and grab a bite to eat. Bennett would kill me since I've enjoyed fast food joints for three straight days, but I swear that will change. After our gluttony, we hit one of our houses, whichever one is closer to where we ate, for a quick shower, change of clothes, and it's off to work.

By shift's end, we're planning our night, and twice that's meant Jennifer and her friends already. I'm not sure how I feel about this, especially since I know I'm not part of Jennifer's future, but at least we're having fun bowling and playing mini-golf. Unfortunately, dinner has occurred after midnight when we finish, and that means the Diner, but at least I've been ordering chicken and salads–avoiding the mozzarella sticks and nachos. By the time I creep through the front door some time after one, Mom's left the obligatory note reminding me to lock up.

This lifestyle affords no family time. When I wake up, Mom's at work, Layne's at camp, and Mark's interning. Layne landed a junior camp counselor job through the town and he's got a great personality for it. Mark, the economist, refused to have a 'pointless' job in his words, so he's working for free for some local bank's home office in New Haven. He talks about the opportunity and all that jazz, but come fall he'll be begging Mom and Dad for money. Since all of them get up so early, they're in bed when I come home and we only communicate through notes and text messages.

Margaret gave both of us Saturday's off so I'll have to see how they play out. And Sunday's are still my normal school year shift. Since I'm home by dinner hour on Sunday's, Mom made me promise I'd come home and spend the night with the family. I can agree to that.

June 22, 2002

On my day off, I'm up early. Realizing that house is still asleep, I tiptoe out the front door and run a new route, actually an easier route since I'll be on my feet all day.

Forrest is in my drive way at 7:30 and the house is still silent. I leave a note for Mom saying I won't be back until midnight or so and dart out the door. By 7:45 we have Jennifer and Lisa and we're New London bound.

Last night we caught the forecast at the diner and the weatherman said sunny and low 80's at the beaches. And that's when the light bulb went off. One of my destinations for the summer was flashing in my head. Block Island. I nervously proposed the idea to the table, and they all immediately agreed. Turns out none of us had ever been, but we all wanted to go. Dropping off Jennifer a bit later, we discovered the ferry left New London at 9:00 in the morning and 3:00 in the afternoon. We wanted to spend the day, not the night, so we committed to the morning departure. As we left Jennifer's she promised to print out maps of Block Island, bike rental locations, and things to do.

We pull in to the ferry terminal just before 8:30; it's packed and I'm fearing we needed reservations. By 8:40 we've made it to the front of the ticket line. Luckily the agent informs us they have a dozen or so tickets left and we hop on four and are immediately called for boarding. The sky is flawless and we rocket to the top deck, hoping to enjoy the breeze and see the coast fade along the journey. Waiting for departure, my cell phone rings and the caller ID says Dad.

"Fuck," I mutter to myself.

"What's wrong?" Jennifer inquires.

"It's my dad's day today."

"Hello."

"Andrew, it's your father, how are you pal."

"Good Dad, how are you?"

"Fine, just seeing what time you and your brothers were coming up. I didn't call the house in case someone was sleeping, but I figured you'd be up and running, no pun intended, by now."

My conscience was throbbing. I know my Dad looks forward to spending Saturdays with me, and I know he'll be devastated. "Well," I stammer, "I'm kind of on a ferry to Block Island right now. I sort of forgot that this was your day. I'm sorry."

"Oh, well umm, so I guess I won't see you today. But that's ok pal, I want you to enjoy your time with your friends. I know you worked all week, so maybe we can get together next Saturday." Dad's tone said it all. The cheerful bounce in his voice from the initial hello crashed into a sorrowful acceptance by the time he hung up.

And I can tell by the way Jennifer is looking at me that she thinks I'm going to sink into depression and ruin the trip. Because I do feel bad, and I don't like to hurt people.

"No worries," Forrest chimes in. "If he wants to see you, he knows where you live, remember, he left you, it's not your responsibility."

And he's right. Dad left. He doesn't feel bad the countless nights a week that I come home and he doesn't. Forrest's philosophy is perfect and I smile, pull my camera and snap a shot of Forrest, Lisa, and Jennifer huddled over the edge. Right after the click, the gentle sea noises are splintered by the ferry's horn announcing departure, a few minutes late, but that's alright. I hope the captain knows he's cutting into our island time. According to the schedule, it's a one hour ride, so we should be there at 10:04 now. I hate tardiness. Damn Bennett, another thing he taught me.

It's funny how the distance on the water never seems to come closer, yet the past disappears so rapidly. Within the first couple minutes of the voyage, I capture the fleeting New London coastline and downtown on film, but now only the gray of the Sound and the blue of the sky provide scenery. At 10:03 we dock. The day has begun.

Our first order of business was to snag bikes for the day. Cheap and somewhat reliable, we headed straight for the famous lighthouse on the north side of the island. For most of the ride, the wind hit us straight on and we were surprised how tired we were upon arrival. The countless steps to the top of the lighthouse didn't help. My lungs were fine, but for some reason, my legs weren't: so much for all of my cross country training. We snapped a few photographs from the top; on one side we thought we could look clear across to Long Island, but it was probably an illusion or our wanting eyes playing tricks on us. The better view came from the opposite side, as we could literally see the entire island. Cars moved like ants scurrying for a hiding place while brown bodies ran to and from the rolling waves.

Our map of Block Island highlighted the fact that few roads were paved, being the daredevils that we are, we decided to take the scenic ride back into town: a dirt road. Unfortunately, the bikes we had rented weren't the best for this type of terrain and despite having the wind at our back, our pace slackened considerably. It was tough not to laugh when Jennifer slowed down so much that she literally fell over sideways when she swerved off the road into the grass. I snapped a picture, which she didn't seem to appreciate too much, but in good time she too was laughing. None of us were laughing when Forrest popped a tire and we had to walk the last mile or so. Scared of what the fine would be, we purchased a tube in town and changed the tire ourselves.

We rejuvenated ourselves with lunch–cafes all over downtown, ditched our bikes, and walked through town. Wherever I go, I buy t-shirts, and today was no different. Since I couldn't decide which one I liked, I bought three: one featuring a map of the island, one featuring a light house, and one simply saying 'Block Island.' These can sit on my shelf with the countless other t-shirts I own, but barely wear. After town, we strolled over to the beach and I was amazed at how much cooler the water was compared to home. Instead of swimming, we dug a hole. We tried to make it six feet deep, but the lifeguard cut us off around four feet. After we filled it in, we had no use for the beach and decided to bike to the south side of the island for more scenery and another light house–this time using only paved roads. The scenery, though beautiful, proved repetitive and the second lighthouse disappointed when compared to the first. But on our way back we spotted a couple of turtles just off the road. We took pictures, then made sure they safely made it to the pond across the way, which we assumed was their destination.

By the time we made it back to town, it was was nearly five o'clock and we opted for this ferry seeing how the next one wouldn't be until eight. The motion of the water certainly relaxed our bodies, perhaps helping us feel just how exhausted we were. By the time we reached New London, we were all laconic robots. We didn't even bother with dinner, instead, Jennifer and Lisa went home as did Forrest and I. Home by ten, only Mom was there. Layne and Mark were spending the night at Dad's and Mom had a dirty look for me when I came in. But I told her Forrest's philosophy, and she just smiled at me knowingly.

Perhaps she's felt this way for a while.

June 26, 2002

Mark took the day off of work so that he and I could have some brotherly bonding time; he claims we've never had enough of that. I was lucky enough to find someone to cover my shift. At first, I was going to end our brother day at mid afternoon and go to work, but that pissed him off, so I conceded that if he took a full day, so would I. The catch being, of course, he doesn't lose any money from his unpaid internship while I lose a day's wages. But whatever, according to Mom I can spare one day for my brother.

The cool part was that Mark let me pick the itinerary. So I suggested New York City. At first, he laughed at my idea, but when I pointed out that it was less than two hours on the train to midtown Manhattan and we could see Times Square, Central Park, Ground Zero, Empire State Building, Rockefeller Center, countless museums, and so on, he agreed. We boarded the 7:48 train and arrived in Grand Central just before 10:00. Mark insisted on the financial district, which I acquiesced given that we were here in the first place. So after trudging past countless buildings that I could care less about on Wall Street, we decided on Times Square for lunch and actually ended up scoring tickets for tonight's taping of Conan O'Brien, even though I'd never heard of any of the guests, just being there was awesome.

After lunch, I dragged Mark through the Met and Guggenheim, which I know drove him crazy. But I guess we were even: he had the financial district, I had the art district. The walk between the two museums is spectacular. A tree lined street guides you to the destinations, behind one side rests Central Park. We only had time to hit a couple of the park highlights, but I know I'll be back there again someday. It's now on my list. Just outside the museums, countless artists and photographers as well as small merchants had kiosks set up. I insisted on rummaging through countless prints until I found three–that was the special, three for twenty dollars or eight dollars each. Mark grabbed a soda and waited impatiently for me, but I found Central Park, the Brooklyn Bridge, and the skyline to take home with me. Mark took a plastic bottle.

The taping of Conan was done by seven, and we hit a corner pizza shop for dinner. I thought we'd probably be readying ourselves for home, but Mark suggested going to the top of the Empire State Building. What a great idea. I'm sure Mark was focusing on the building's economic impact while I couldn't wait to see the city as the sunset. By the time we bought our tickets and made it to the top, there was just a hint of sun left. To the east facing side of the overlook, the city was lit by artificial light and the neon colors contrasted awkwardly with the soft hues below. On the west side, the sun's light was still winning the battle, though barely, as shadows traced imposing figures across the buildings and streets below. Every second, as darkness took over, a new neighborhood lit up until ever so slowly, darkness had completely swallowed the sun, but it was no match for manmade light. I snapped scores of photographs and even had a tourist snap one of Mark and I just before the sun escaped. I think both Mark and I enjoyed this part of the day the most, even if for two separate reasons.

July 1, 2002

Jennifer spends most of her summer days working at a day camp for elementary school students. She rarely is able to hang at the beach with us. And despite the ambiguity of our current relationship, I'm grateful she wasn't here today.

I'm sure we're both free to date other people, and I'm sure I'd rage if Jennifer started seeing somebody. Just like she'd probably do the same to me. And therein lies the essential problem in our relationship: we're friends who are not dating, but would be shattered if one of us hooked up with somebody else.

The courts were oddly packed for a Monday. Usually the weekend requires waiting, but I guess with the holiday coming up, many families took the whole week off. Forrest and I had pretty much given up on finding court space, when two complete strangers eyed us. They didn't look familiar, but one of them said he saw me play last summer–he recognized my bleach blonde hair and piercings. Though I've never thought that either were defining characteristics, the truth is that in a clean cut rich preppy town such as ours, I can stick out some. Not that I'm sloppy, sure my hair flops a little, but it's not shaggy. And I'm certainly not a poster boy for piercing, only two hoops–one in each ear. But around the courts, I'm the only guy with a piercing, let alone two.

Forrest and I eagerly agreed to pair up with them. They had a foursome. But the two hour court wait drove a couple of them away. We'd have to fill-in. It turns out our new partners were part of the population of my town that I generally hate: visitors. Every summer they crash our town, some for a day, many for a week or two, and others for the whole summer. Craig and Miles come every year for a week or two with their parents from New Jersey. They seem to be my age and are running from the daily monotony of hanging with their extended family. I don't think I noticed just how crowded the courts were until after our first game. We won; and literally hundreds of people cheered, though I think some of the cheering came from the fact that we had just beaten a team that had owned the court for quite a while. Craig and Miles were pretty good, apparently they make it to the Jersey shore from time to time and picked up a few games.

We lost our third game, to a local team that gave us trouble even when Forrest and I played with the best partners our town had to offer. Without the common timing of some of our other partners, we were goners with Miles and Craig flanking us. Knowing we wouldn't get anymore court time, I was about ready to call it an early day before work, when I noticed several girls I'd never seen before walking towards Craig and Miles. I eyed myself–running my hands through my hair, wiping sweat and sand away–and aimlessly wandered in their direction pretending to have a purpose.

"Hey," I intoned toward Miles, "thanks for the game today. You guys around all week?"

"Yeah," he replied, "our whole family is here for the week."

"Well at least you and Craig got to bring your girlfriends," I clandestinely tried to figure some things our."

"I wish," Miles laughed, "my parents would never let us do that. If you're talking about Kelcey and Tara," he pointed just in front of him, "they're our cousins."

I laughed, as did Craig, Miles, Tara, Kelcey, and Forrest, who finally decided to join the fray. Knowing I still had plenty of time before work, I asked them to come into town for a bite to eat. They all happily obliged and six of us crammed into Forrest's Jeep sitting all over each other; luckily town was just a mile away.

I didn't really know what I was doing, but Tara was beautiful. She was not at all like Jennifer in that she had brown hair and brown eyes as well as being shorter, but I found her stunningly attractive. Throughout the entire time we spent in town, I tried to finagle myself so that the two of us were always next to each other. I let her do most of the talking (I generally find the more I talk, the worse off I am). And by the time work hour rolled around, I was at a definite crossroads, call in sick and convince Tara to spend the night with me, or go to work and leave her behind.

But tonight, Fate smiled kindly upon me, as the daunting hour approached, Tara talked of a necessary family dinner. I told her of my work shift and inquired about her late night availability. It turns out, that Fate was going to be pulling for both of us.

After work, Forrest dropped me off at Tara's beach house. She was waiting outside and just the two of us strolled the beach. For a short time, we held each other's hand and gently kissed beneath the moon lit skies. Despite the moment, a part of me didn't feel right. She wasn't as familiar as Jennifer had once been, yet her difference felt indifferent.

A few minutes later, I knew why. Tara was looking for a good time and I was just the vehicle she was looking for.

"So where's the party tonight?"

"What do you mean," I replied.

"Well, I figured we'd be hanging out with your friends and having some fun tonight. I told Craig and Miles we'd call them and let them know where to meet us."

"Tara," I began, "I'm here with you tonight because I wanted to be with you, not to crash somebody's party. In fact, I don't even drink. If you're looking for that, then you have to find somebody else to hangout with."

And that's when the guilt and awkwardness began. Clearly, Tara wanted no part of me, except the part that could take her to a party; the very part of me that no longer existed. And here I felt I actually found somebody cool, but I discovered I hadn't. In fact, I knew that Jennifer would never ask me to take her to some party. And within a few minutes, I walked Tara home, and myself just a few minutes later.

I stayed home for the rest of the night playing guitar. Despite the numerous songs I began to strum, mostly I found myself thinking of songs for Jennifer and longing for her. I promised myself that I would let her be, but also that I would win her over. Somehow a combination like that seems destined to fail.

It had failed once already.

July 4, 2002

Even though the grocery store is open normal hours today–so much for celebrating the Fourth– I don't have to work, which makes me so happy. Forrest and I begged Margaret to give us this day off. She broke out the whole seniority thing and how she'd have to find two people to cover our shifts on a holiday. I volunteered Margaret pointing out she'd taken off more than her share of Sundays that she was supposed to work not to mention a four day holiday weekend for Memorial Day. Margaret didn't find my suggestion amusing. But Forrest and I persisted noting that unlike so much of the 'tenured' help, we never call out 'sick' at the last minute nor do we show up late. Margaret did concede that our attendance record is excellent, though she understandably stopped short of declaring our job performance as being exemplary. After much begging, she finally agreed to give us both the day off, though she said we owed her one. My smart ass told her that I'll take it off the four you owe from May.

I'll leave this topic in a second, but I find it amusing that Margaret took my suggestion and is signed up to cashier today, the other cashier is a single mom who was grateful for the chance to work a double since it meant twelve hours of work, double pay since it's a holiday. Today, she'll make what she normally makes in four days and not have to pay for a baby sitter since her own mom has the day off. Things always have a way of working themselves out I guess.

With this day off, I'm fulfilling another one of my summer activities: Ocean Beach, New London. We are the same fantastic foursome that went to Block Island in June, only today our chemistry and destinations are different. Since I realized that Jennifer was no guarantee to be by my side through thick and thin, I decided that she and I would be friends. I never declared this to her, but I think by the way we've both been acting that it's something that doesn't need to be stated. On the other hand, Lisa and Forrest are trying to move beyond the friend stage. But they're awkward; every time they schedule alone time, miraculously my phone or Jennifer's (sometimes both) rings before the end of the night and they find a way to lose their alone time. Forrest and I chatted about this, he says she gets nervous and doesn't want to rush things, so he says they have pressure free dates where they just hangout alone for a while and end the night with friends to prevent uncomfortable goodbyes. Lisa tells Jennifer a different story, however. Lisa claims that every time she and Forrest start to get close, he backs away saying he doesn't want her to do something she'll regret and it would be better to wait a little while longer. Given that Forrest is a sixteen year old male, I think Lisa's story is pathetic and she's covering her own insecurities.

By nine o'clock we've already arrived at Ocean Beach, and the beach is still pretty empty, but we claim a grill and picnic table that will last us for the day. Unspoken rules regarding these things go a long way; we just pray that nobody moves our stuff while we're hitting the beach, but again, these types of rules go a long way and have withstood the test of time. We duly note that several other grills and tables have been claimed without visible human occupants, just charcoal, table cloths, chairs, coolers, and other assorted items.

We decide to toss the frisbee on the beach before it becomes too crowded and the sand too hot. I spend most of the time looking at two things: Jennifer and myself, which helps to explain my pathetic frisbee performance. At first, I was looking singularly at Jennifer, and thinking how amazing she looks in a bikini. It was clear she'd spent considerable time perfecting her tan and that track season had left her in good shape. Her blonde streaked hair swaying rhythmically at the ocean, and her smile drawing me into her all over again. And as I picked up the frisbee that landed at my feet, I started looking at myself, in two ways, physically and socially. Physically, I too looked good (if I must say), my six pack abs, sinewy strength, and a good tan, though still a bit of a farmer's. Then the social me, how can I still be obsessing over Jennifer? She wants to be friends and it's clear, but I can't move past it, even though I thought I could. So I stop looking at both of us and absently watch the frisbee sail through the hazy sunshine, landing in other people's beach blankets, disturbing their morning. And with that, frisbee ends.

The rest of the morning we split between body surfing the waves, swimming, sunbathing, and the other typical beach stuff. Ocean Beach is known for its waves, so it was nice to just watch them crash, foam, and recede; I captured quite a few pictures of this phenomenon. We strolled the boardwalk for a few minutes, but found nothing to truly amuse us.

Partially bored, partially dehydrated, approaching sunburnt status, we take a hiatus from the beach, leaving our provisions behind. Just a few minutes down the road is Mystic Seaport and aquarium. Now just past noon, the town is packed. We hit the Seaport first and tour some of the historic ships, which was exceedingly cool, and refrain from buying the cheesy souvenirs. After an hour or so we seek refuge in the aquarium. Here, we stop talking and just mosey through the exhibits, enjoying the air-conditioning, chugging bottles of water, and staring blankly at the aquatic life. I snap pictures of the exhibits and try to capture one of us in each picture. No matter who I photograph, a zombie appears on the screen of my digital camera. The sun has already taken its toll on us and we haven't even made it to fireworks yet. On the way out of the aquarium, we all succumb to the overpriced snow cones and experience brain freezes of every magnitude. But the snow cones revive us and when we return to the beach we are revved up about cooking. Luckily no one stole our provisions, though we're obviously amateurs seeing how nobody thought to bring matches or a lighter to start the fire. Thankfully every other person on earth came more prepared than us and we easily find a family willing to spare several matches.

Cooking is a group effort. We brought tons more food than we needed, but when you work at a grocery store that shouldn't be a surprise. We grill chicken, burgers, hotdogs, veggie burgers, corn on the cob, and eggplant. Plus we brought two huge containers of fruit salad and potato salad, and a watermelon to slice up. For some reason we also brought scores of juices and sodas, most of which we hadn't touched despite the heat. Though we are inexperienced, our spread rivals anybody's at the beach. We decide to cook all the meat since we don't know what else to do with it; but we brought enough for everybody to have two of everything, which just wasn't going to happen. So with a dozen or so mixed products left, we put them on a tray at the end of our picnic table with a sing that reads "Free, Just Cooked Too Much." With in five minutes, passerbys claim every last morsel, most of whom say thanks, and a few who compliment the chefs.

By the time we finish with clean-up, it's approaching seven, but we still have two hours until fireworks and none of us feel like swimming, playing in the sand, or moving. So we simply turn on the radio, find a decent station, and talk about nothing. At times during the conversation my mind wanders to mostly the same two topics: Jennifer and me, Lisa and Forrest. I wonder who else's mind is wandering and as the sun makes a picture perfect exit that my camera can't quite duplicate, I wonder just where the sun will rise on all of us as the sands of time blow our futures.

We decide to relay our blankets on the beach for the fireworks and kill the music. The heat has subsided some, but it's still hot out so I know I can't put my arm around Jennifer pretending to keep her warm.

Reds, blues, greens, whites illuminate the sky in array of shapes, silencing the beach crowd. The fireworks are coming from a barge off in the water, and behind us on the boardwalk a band plays patriotic songs choreographed specifically for tonight. Perfect. And unexpectedly Jennifer snuggles in close to me and kisses me on the cheek. Confused, I don't kiss her back, but just hold her close as the grand finale concludes to a ridiculous round of applause. I've never quite understood why people clap after the fireworks, no one can hear you, it's almost as stupid as clapping in the movies, it's not like the actors are there to say thank you. But I keep these comments to myself.

Walking back to Forrest's car, I gently take Jennifer's hand, which she readily welcomes and we lag behind Lisa and Forrest who aren't talking and walk at least an arm's length apart. Against a tree, I nudge Jennifer up against it and kiss her passionately, she reciprocates, but given the public nature of our display, we end quickly and sit together in the back of Forrest's car. Throughout the ride home, we sit close, kissing from time to time, saying very little.

"What's up with you and Lisa?" I ask Forrest after dropping the girls off.

"Nothing. Why?"

"That's what I thought. But I mean something could totally be there if you wanted it to be."

Forrest doesn't say anything in response for several seconds, then blurts out, "I don't know, she's cool and all, but it's like dating my little cousin, she's just so innocent. Every time I kissed her when we were alone last week, I felt guilty." He changes the subject quickly, "What's up with you and Jennifer?"

"That, my friend, I wish I knew. One minute we're friends, the next we're on two totally separate wave lengths, the next we're inseparable. I'm sure a good talk is coming tomorrow."

Quietly, I wonder which one of us will initiate it and just where it will go; I know where I want it to go, but I'm afraid Jennifer doesn't.

July 5, 2002

But the talk isn't from Jennifer. Instead it's from my parents, both of them, so I know this can't be good. Given the holiday on Thursday, both Mom and Dad were lucky enough to secure a four day weekend.

By 8:00 in the morning, Dad has already completed the drive to Mom's house and they've both decided to wait for me in the living room knowing that I'll be preparing for my morning run any second now.

"Dad?" I mumble as I come into the living room. I have no clue why he's in Mom's house so early.

"Son," he begins and with the mere word 'son,' I feel dread, but I can't seem to fathom what I've done that is so heinous, "we need to talk, all of us, you, me, your mother."

"Ok, what happened?"

Mom chimes in, "I asked your father to be here because I'm concerned about how you don't spend anytime with your family. You're never home here. You haven't seen your father all summer, and yesterday you didn't even bother coming to the cookout I had with your brothers, neighbors, and friends."

"I told you I had plans and couldn't make it." I'm already feeling defensive and sense a war coming on.

"Andrew," Dad's turn, "it's like you don't want spend time with Lois and me plus Devin look so forward to you coming up."

"Well Dad, I didn't move out so there's the solution to that problem." And suddenly I'm using Forrest's philosophy as my weapon, justification, and defense.

"NO!" Dad thunders, "we're talking about the present, not ten years ago."

"Twelve," I correct him.

"Andrew," back to Mom, "I leave for work and you're sleeping, all day I can't get a hold of you because you're at the beach playing, then after work you stay out until all hours of the night. The only time I see you is when I go to the grocery store. And Andrew, please, your father has always looked out for you, the least you can do is talk about the present with him."

"Fine. Here's the present. Mom, I live here. When you come home from work at five, I'm at work, even if I came home right at ten when I get off, you'd be thirty minutes from bed. So I'll see to it that I stop by home for thirty minutes. When you leave for work at seven, knock on my door and I'll say good morning..."

"Andrew," she tries interrupting, but I won't be deterred.

"Dad," I ignore the interruption, "I live here, in the present. You live an hour away. My school, job, friends, and home are here, still in the present. You live an hour away, where I don't have a job, I don't go to school, and I don't have any friends. In fact, I don't even have a bedroom at your house; I sleep on a fold out couch in the living room, sometimes with a brother. Let's talk about the present. If you'd like me to quit my job, drop out of school, and lose all my friends, then by all means lets transfer my present to one hour away."

"So that's what this is all about, the divorce?" Dad asks with some sincerity in his voice, not the caustic tone I was expecting in reply.

And he's right, at least about his part. My life is here, not where he lives, and I don't feel it's my responsibility to change the present he created for me, that's his responsibility. But Mom's a different story, up until this summer, I'd always been home more, and I know she's upset we don't spend time together, and I know in my heart that I need to do something about that, but for some reason I'm not ready to concede this point.

So instead, I explain, "I'm going to go running in a few minutes, before it gets too hot. But first, I'm writing down my schedule so that while I'm running you two can figure out how to make things work.

I create a chart which clearly shows free time until 4:00pm Monday through Friday, starring one hour as an exception for running. After 4:00 until 10:00pm I pencil in work, then free time for the rest of the night. On Saturday I note that I have the day off, but I also note that I'd like at least either the day or night to myself since it's my only off day. Finally, I note that I work all day on Sunday, but I'm free at night. At the end of the page I remind them that I'll be gone July 13th through July 28th with Bennett. I hand the slip to my parents, grab my shoes, and bolt.

Running usually clears my head. But not today, part of me felt bad about what just transpired and the attitude I conveyed. Part of me is pissed at Dad for pressuring me like this, especially since never once has he ever been around to ask how school was, but now he's hurt because I missed a couple of father-son days. Where was he for twelve years? Mom surprises me, I thought she'd be happy that I have friends again, but perhaps she feels it's at her expense.

So by the time I finish my 60 minute jaunt, I'm scared to walk through the door because I don't know how I'm going to react, let alone my parents.

"How about you and I hit the mall tomorrow and we'll pick-up what you need for your trip with Mr. Bennett," Dad begins. "Make a list, and we'll see what we can find. Then we'll grab some lunch and find something to do for a few hours in the afternoon. That way you can have Saturday night to yourself."

"Cool, we have to meet around eleven, though, I go for my driver's license at 10:00."

"How about I'll make sure you're there at ten."

"Deal."

"And Andrew, all I want is a family dinner. All I'm asking for is Sundays. I want Sundays. After work, come home, I'll either cook or we'll go out, the family. And after dinner I want to do something, you know, rent a movie, play a game, anything," Mom requests.

"No problem. You know, it's not like I don't like you guys. It's just that our work schedules are opposites."

"I know," Mom contributes, "but I don't like how late you stay out at night, I would like you home earlier."

"I don't drink anymore and I don't do drugs."

"Anymore?" Dad picked up on a word I probably shouldn't have used.

"Before Harris died, I used to party with them, I'm pretty sure Mom suspected it, but I think I hid it pretty good. But now you know. Since he died, I haven't partied once. That's sort of how I lost so many of my friends, but I've found some new ones, well a few at least."

"You knew about him partying?" Dad accuses Mom.

"Oh so did we when we were his age, I just thought so long as he wasn't driving around with people who were drinking that he'd be better off than me forbidding him to go out. Plus I wasn't even sure if he was partying, but he doesn't now and I know that for a fact."

"See you tomorrow Dad," I say as Forrest pulls into the driveway for our beach trip.

"Where are you going," Mom screams.

"The beach, I thought I agreed to the schedule and nothing's scheduled now."

"You need to cut the lawn before you go to work."

"Fine!" I scream hopping into Forrest's car and tell him I can only stay until two, but no matter, we're getting an earlier start since it's a holiday weekend.

July 6, 2002

Having already passed the written part of the exam, all I had to do was pass the road portion and I would be a fully certified driver–sort of, I'd have to obey passenger capacity limits as well restricted driving after midnight for a few months. Which sort of started me wondering, doesn't Forrest break that rule almost everyday and night? Probably one of those things that isn't enforced unless you're pulled over for something else; I wonder if my parents are even aware that these laws exist. I hope not.

One fault of my father is that he's on time to a fault. So I certainly wasn't surprised to see him bright and early Saturday morning ready to go. Driving over to the test facility, we didn't talk about much, mostly Dad tried to remind me about looking both ways and coming to complete stops. I was just hoping I wouldn't have to parallel park, otherwise I thought I'd be fine, though my perspiring hands and body seemed to suggest otherwise.

Thankfully, appointments are required for a driver's test, so we didn't have to wait in the ridiculously long line that seems to be a trademark of every motor vehicle department. A few minutes after ten and the test administrator and I were ready to go. I did everything by the book, including checking my mirrors and looking around the outside of the car for possible objects. Once inside the car, I reminded the instructor to buckle up, after all, passengers riding in the front seat of a motor vehicle must be properly secured, regardless of age. He told me that very few teens remember that and usually lose a point for not asking him to buckle up.

I think this impressed him, seeing how my road test lasted five minutes. We left the parking lot, turned right down the first side street, made a three point turn, then returned to the parking lot. He told me to park anywhere, so I purposely parked between two cars, thus guaranteeing I'd be in the space. Once parked, he told me to sit here a minute while he finished filling out the form.

I was convinced I'd failed, he wasn't talking to me and we were only out for five minutes–was I so bad that he just wanted to get back here? No traffic lights, no parallel parking, no lane changes, nothing except a stop sign and a three point turn. But I didn't think I screwed any of those up.

"Congratulation," he began, "you are now a licensed driver. I can tell just by leaving the parking lot who is going to pass and who won't. You knew to tell me to put on a seatbelt and you stopped, looked both ways then proceeded. Some are herky jerky speeding up and braking, you weren't. Plus you didn't have to check left and right a thousand times because you were unsure of yourself. Just drive with common sense and you'll be fine."

"Thanks, I was nervous."

I also didn't have the nerve to tell him that he just paid high praise to a driver who recently planted his mother's car through the garage because he confused 'drive' and 'reverse.'

All day today, I kept expecting Dad to have a talk with me about the family and what was the past, but it never truly came. Instead, we simply went to several stores and purchased odds and ends for the trip: a new duffel bag, extra socks and boxers, sandals, a shower caddy, and the like. He paid for everything, and didn't complain about it, a definite first.

After that, we met up with Lois and Devin and had a cookout at a park nearby. Devin and I joined an ultimate frisbee game while Dad and Lois prepared the meal. I didn't know anybody playing, but it didn't bother me. Perhaps having to start my whole peer group over again this year has erased some of my former social fears. I hope so. After lunch, the four of us canoed part of the lake and creek area around the park. Dad and Lois trailed Devin and me. It was cool, nothing special as Devin and I mostly small talked about life and whatnot while pointing out swimming fish, odd shaped vegetation, and new waterways to explore.

Driving back to Mom's house, I think Dad wanted to begin some kind of dialogue regarding family, but he never truly got started. In the end, he simply reminded me that he's always 'just a phone call away.' I don't think he knows how much I hate that phrase because immediate family should never be so far away, but I just nodded in agreement and that was that. I think we both wanted to believe we were happy, but feared the other was pretending.

July 7, 2007

As soon as I walked in the door from work, I could smell the food. Mom knows that I love her porcupine meatballs and I was ready to walk straight to the stove and steal a bite before dinner, except Mom anticipated that and threatened me with food poisoning from undercooked meat–that did the trick. I also knew that tonight's meal was prepared specifically for me. Part of our 'contract' included Sunday dinners and family time, so I immediately recognized Mom's meal was a means of winning me over. And it worked. The food was spectacular.

At first, it was kind of awkward; this was the first time all summer that Mark, Layne, Mom, and I sat at the same table. I figured the three of them had shared several meals together, but with my work and play schedule, I never joined them. The awkward part was Mom trying to force discussions centered around me. She wanted me to feel included, that was clear. At the same time, I hate 'me' centered discussions and kept trying to steer the discussion towards Mark's internship or Layne's feelings about starting at the high school. Whether intentional or unintentional, Mark broke the tension by catching his sleeve on fire when reaching for seconds, but forgetting the burning candle in the middle of the table. Which was odd, the candle I mean, and Mark's sleeves, after all it was still daylight in the middle of summer, why a candle? Why sleeves? But after a brief scare, a laugh from all but Mark, and an angry realization that his 50 dollar shirt was ruined, the tension broke. For the rest of the meal we reminisced about other family mishaps, including Mom accidentally stabbing Layne in the arm when she tried saving a misdirected potato from rolling off the table–once Layne left the emergency room, he and Mom made peace. We also recalled Mom forgetting that she'd left bread in the oven, the flames jogged her memory. Our jovial mood continued into cleanup as we all pitched in with clearing the table, packaging leftovers, doing the dishes, and taking out the trash.

After the meal, we ran around the backyard playing home run derby in our makeshift wiffle ball stadium. Layne won, Mark took second, I finished third, Mom kept score.

And for a short time, I don't think any of us were pretending to be happy.

July 9, 2002

Last night I skipped out on chilling with Forrest after work so I could finish reading *Catch 22*. By three in the morning today, I completed the book Blackwell gave me months ago. Funny, back in the winter I'd finish his books in a few days, now I can barely find time to read. I miss reading and have a list of want-to-reads several pages long, but I also enjoy having friends. My current work, running, and hanging out schedule leaves little time for reading. On the upcoming trip with Bennett, I plan on bringing several books, I'm thinking at night or while traveling there will definitely be some down time.

Today's lunch, though, had little to do with the book, which didn't surprise me too much considering Blackwell and I hadn't talked in almost a month. We met downtown at a great restaurant famous for their wraps, which of course we both ordered: me, southwest turkey; Blackwell, smoked honey ham.

Blackwell began our discourse, "You look great Andrew; you've certainly gotten some sun and been working out."

"Yeah, me and the beach have been friendly this summer."

"The beach and I," Blackwell corrected me, then continued, "but more than anything, I notice a more upbeat person, Andrew."

"Thanks," was all I could reply.

But I was captured by that word 'upbeat.' I hadn't really thought about it, but I was more upbeat and no longer spent countless hours feeling sorry for myself or just downright sad. Mostly, I attributed that to having friends again, a busy schedule, and actually doing some of the things that I promised myself I would do.

I told Blackwell all about our Fourth of July celebration, the trip to Block Island, and the conversation with my parents regarding family time. It was here, family time, that Blackwell perked up.

"So your parents felt left out," Blackwell chimed in.

"I guess so; I understand my mother's perspective, but my dad kind of caught me off guard."

"Well you need to remember that your father would probably like to see more of you, but can't given the situation, so he probably looks forward to the few days you guys do have together and was hurt that you didn't even remember."

"He caused that situation, it's not my fault."

"But that situation didn't involve you, Andrew."

Blackwell angered me with this comment, how could it not involve me, and I spoke my mind. "Mr. Blackwell, with all due respect, that situation did involve me, how could it not?"

"It was between him and your mother; the situation affected you, but did not involve you," Mr. Blackwell attempted to explain.

"Nice try. He chose to leave my mom and in so doing he left me."

"Look at this way, Andrew, despite all of that, hasn't he always been there for you?"

"No."

"How not, Andrew?" Blackwell prodded.

"Every day after school, he's not there to ask about how school went or to simply play a game of catch," and now I felt myself truly becoming angry, and part of my anger was directed at Dad, the rest at Blackwell. I wasn't angry with Blackwell for asking me questions, but rather for not seeing my perspective.

"Andrew, you need to ask yourself about what matters. Being there for your big races when you needed somebody to be there mattered. He was there."

"And so was my mother."

"Good, and he's there whenever you ask him to be somewhere."

"I shouldn't have to ask," but now I knew I was just being argumentative.

"And I shouldn't have to beg you to do your homework, but I do it anyway because I know it will benefit you in the long run."

"This has nothing to do with my homework, and why do you care so much?"

"Because I was just like you," Blackwell began, "I came from divorced parents and spent most of my life hating people, especially my father. I never made peace with the fact that he and my mother had a problem. He never had a problem with me. I did. He died when I was twenty, never knowing how I truly felt."

Suddenly, I knew why Blackwell picked me. He didn't pick me because I liked to read or because I was wasting my potential. He picked me because he saw himself in me. Because he genuinely cared about fixing the past, even if he couldn't fix his own. But I didn't know how to respond, and simply told him I was sorry to hear about his father.

"I don't want you to feel the same way; all I'm asking you to do is to see both sides, that's it Andrew." Perhaps uncomfortable and not sure how close to get, Blackwell changed the subject before I could respond, simply asking, "how was the book."

"Alright, I read most of it last night, but I liked it."

And our conversation drifted from the book to my upcoming trip and eventually to running and classes I'd be taking next year.

By the time we left, our comfort level had largely returned and our heated conversation seemed a distant past, but upon departure, I knew Blackwell had more to say, but he simply said, "Andrew, I'm so happy to see you happy, and I want you to continue to be happy. At the same time, I don't want you to make the same mistake I made. I won't bring this up again unless you want to."

"Ok," was all I could say.

Walking away, I couldn't tell if Blackwell and I were coming closer, or driving a wedge in our relationship. For the longest time, I thought he was trying to be a father figure to me, but I realized that's not what he wanted.

But it is what I wanted. I just couldn't tell him.

July 12, 2002

So here's my philosophy, I took today off of work so that I could pack for the west coast trip. This way, I wouldn't lose beach time and I'd still be able to hangout at night. Mom was happy because we could have dinner together.

The beach was business as normal–volleyball, sun, water, volleyball. And dinner with Mom certainly was nice–Mark was 'working for free' late while Layne was out of town for the weekend on a boat trip with his friend's family. I thought Mom would cook, but she didn't. Instead she took me to an outdoor restaurant right on the water in the next town over. As at most outdoor restaurants, everything was cooked on a fire grill. I ordered salmon while Mom opted for swordfish–we swapped parts of our meals, both were delicious, to say the least. Most of our conversation surrounded my upcoming trip.

But towards the end of the meal, she said something odd, "I know Coach Bennett is looking forward to the trip."

"I'm sure he is," I responded absent mindedly, then I remembered that Mom used the word 'know." I continued, "How do you know he is?"

"Oh, uh, he told me," Mom stumbled through her response, leaving me with some suspicions.

"When?"

"A couple of days ago, I think, he called the house making sure you didn't need anything and that everything was all set," Mom sped through this response with more fluidity and confidence.

"How come you didn't tell me he called; what if I needed something?"

"Well, Andrew, he called at night and you're never home at night plus I don't see you during the day so it must have slipped my mind."

Adequately satisfied about how Mom knew about Bennett's excitement, my unfounded fears quickly abated.

After dinner, I finished packing. I think I packed everything I owned. Not sure of what the weather would be like, I packed not only all of my summer clothes and running clothes, but also rain gear, sweatshirts, fleeces, long pants, hiking boots, and a set of nice clothes, just in case we went somewhere classy. I managed to squeeze all of this into a suitcase and duffle bag. I packed a third bag containing all of my 'small' items: two books, disc player, camera, cd's, cell phone, and my journal.

By the time I finished packing, it was nearly ten o'clock. Minutes later, Forrest was impatiently parked in my driveway. I bolted out of the door and we bolted down the road, though I didn't know where we were going. I tried to coerce information from Forrest, but he clandestinely answered my inquiries as we drove down US-1.

At the edge of town sits this arcade and pool hall. It's not really a true pool hall seeing how it's smoke and alcohol free, but it has a shitloads of arcade games, pool tables, pinball, and the like–the same place Jennifer and I went for Valentine's Day.

"Why are we going here?" I inquired.

"To meet up with somebody," Forrest nonchalantly replied.

"Who?"

"You'll see."

We ambled through the door and moseyed downstairs, where I found Jennifer, Lisa, and a few of our volleyball teammates. Jennifer held matches in her hand and lit the candles on a cake, shaped like a runner. After I blew out the candles, I read the printing: *Run like the wind, we'll hear you in the breeze*.

I loved it; I had no idea that I was getting a going away party. As the night wore on, it was clear that Jennifer had organized the whole shindig, which only made things more difficult. I spent most of my time between pool shots contemplating not only how I would say goodbye to Jennifer, but also who she was to me. I thought she had made it clear that we were friends, and though I wanted more, I wasn't sure if she did, and I was certainly tired of the changing feelings she had for me. I needed to know where we were now, and where we were going.

So as the evening began to head towards closure, I purposefully sat alone and watched Forrest and Lisa flirt with each other in the plastic ball pool o' fun. I knew Jennifer would come over and see me.

"Hey," I casually acknowledged her presence.

"So why are you sitting all by yourself."

"I don't know," I lied, "I was just thinking about how much I'm going to miss everybody and how weird these next couple of weeks are going to be."

"Are you going to miss me?" Jennifer was getting right to the point, perhaps she was reading my mind and knew what I really wanted to talk about.

"Yeah," I played it cool, but immediately spilled my deck, "but I was thinking more about if you would miss me."

"Andrew," Jennifer began, "of course I'm going to miss you. I know Lisa will be around, but I'm not sure if Forrest and her will just hangout or if I'll be a third wheel, or whatever."

And suddenly, I was feeling used. Was I only Jennifer's sidekick so she wouldn't feel like a third wheel, was she really this self motivated?

"So you're worried about who you'll hangout with since I won't be readily available?" I overly simplified.

I expected a tumultuous response, instead she calmly replied, "I'm worried about what I'll feel when you're gone. I know we go through phases, but at night when I'm alone and wishing somebody was with me, you're the only one I want."

She said it, the words I'd been waiting all year to hear, I wanted to dance in celebration, but I held myself in check, merely saying, "I've been feeling that way about you for a long time."

Jennifer and I held each other for the rest of the night; we both knew we wouldn't be able to share any alone time, but when Forrest dropped her off, I walked her to the door and we made whispered promises to each other, culminating in a gentle kiss goodbye, but it was what both of us believed would be a new beginning.

July 13, 2002

Bennett should be here any minute now. He's going to leave his car at my house then Mom is going to drop us off at the train station. I'm anxious. So much so that I'm sweating and can feel drops of perspiration dripping down my sides. I guess for most people, this type of sweat gets caught in their armpit hair, but not me. Though you may find it weird, I shave my underarms. I read an article about it a running magazine a few months back. So many runners swore by shaved armpits, I just had to try it. And now I'm addicted. Aside from the smoothness factor, it makes running a more pleasurable experience. I used to get rashes that would sting my underarms and experience a perpetual stickiness while running. But not anymore. While running, nothing inhibits my flow, sweat simply flows down my body and eventually gravity does its thing, it doesn't get caught anywhere. But now, I wish I had a layer to catch my sweat.

I'm not scared of Bennett, it's just different. I worried all night about what we would talk about and how we would interact. I'm not sure if I'll be able to write in my journal in front of him. I can't even do it in front of my own mother, instead, I close my bedroom door and do it alone. But on this trip, I wonder if I'll even have a moment of alone time, I wonder if I'll end up disappointing Bennett or if we'll walk away from this experience wishing it had never happened.

July 15, 2002

It's dark and raining, most passengers find this not to be the best time for sightseeing, I practically have the car to myself. Bennett is back in our sleeper and I have a moment to gather my thoughts on paper.

These last couple of days have been cool; the train ride to Chicago was largely uneventful, but we had a few hours to explore Chicago before our connecting train arrived. Bennett thought Navy Pier would be a worthwhile adventure, and we hopped a speed boat ride giving us a tour of the Chicago skyline from the lake, totally worth the price.

The first night on the Seattle train was an experience. It was totally packed and we shared a dinner table with an older couple traveling to see their grandchildren for the first time. After dinner we hit the sightseer car, which was equally packed as people crowded for the best view of the sunset, moon rising, and stars emerging. Later, a movie played in another car, but there was a greater demand than expected so not everybody had a seat. I'd already seen the movie and gave up my seat to a girl not much older than me. Bennett did the same and we headed back to our room and read our books. Sleeping the first night on the Chicago train was hard for many reasons. First, I don't sleep well around strangers, never have, but usually after a night or two I adjust. Second, the bed is understandably small and I had trouble with the perpetual rocking of the train. But last night, I slept much better and had numerous dreams involving movement.

Tonight is our last night on the train as we'll be in Seattle in the morning. So far, it's been what I expected, I guess. I thought I might meet more people, but I guess to most people I'm just a kid who loves trains.

There's been quite a bit of quiet time that I've largely spent reading or thinking about home. Though I miss my family, I spend most of my time thinking about Jennifer. Mom gave me a new cell phone to take on the trip, and I've thought about calling Jennifer a dozen times or so, but that's something her boyfriend would do and I'm not her boyfriend, or am I? Until recently, I thought we'd bridged that gap, but Friday night blew that theory up. I repeatedly dwell on what to bring her back. Part of me thinks I should look for the perfect gift that she'll fall for, the other part of me wants to opt for the conventional tourist shop gift. I guess I should wait until the very end of the trip to buy her something, by that time maybe my thoughts will be clearer. But knowing me, they'll only be foggier.

By the way, did I mention that I'm reading again, it's this book called *Last Wave* and it's about a surfer whose contemplating a surgery to ease the pain in his foot while at the same time falling in love with his best friend's sister. Though not exactly similar to my story, his mixed up feelings for a girl who sends him mixed signals strikes home readily; I can't wait to see how this turns out, perhaps it will help me out some.

July 22, 2002

Even if I wasn't terrified of writing in front of Bennett, I wouldn't have had the time to. Every minute of everyday is full of adventure. So far we've explored Seattle, Takoma, Olympia and Portland, hiked through Mt. Rainer Park, Olympic National Forrest, and the Columbia River Gorge, attempted to surf in Seaside, drove through Mt. Hood and now we've landed at Crater Lake. We're crashing a few miles away in Klamath Falls, Bennett's out grabbing some takeout, I decided to wait back here at the hotel, so I could write for a few minutes.

We don't waste daylight. And by the time we hit our lodging for the night, all there's left to do is shower and mercifully fall asleep. At the end of each day I'm exhausted, but everyday brings new adventures and a greater sense of awe. Seeing the Pacific Ocean for the first time was insane; cliffs dwelled literally feet from the sand while waves crashed across rocks jutting hundreds of feet into the water.

I know I'm flying through this and leaving out most every detail, but I need to finish before Bennett returns, maybe in time I won't feel awkward writing in front of him. In fact, I'm kind of surprised I feel strange about it because we've jelled really well; though most of our conversation has surrounded running and the day's activities, even in long silences during the drives, it's cool. We just listen to the music and enjoy the scenery, at times one of us pointing out a sight. Like coming into town today and watching the setting sun blaze the sky with reds and oranges. We pulled over for photographs, then resumed our contented silence until we hit the hotel.

The long silences have also given me time to think about who I am and what I want. Of course that means lots of thinking about Jennifer, but surprisingly, I think very little about my past, most of my thoughts focus on the future. And I guess that's a good thing. The next trick is figuring out just what I think.

July 28, 2002

So much has happened this week that I haven't even thought about writing, until now. Bennett and I just finished running the race here in San Francisco; he's chilling in the hotel's pool, but I just showered and decided to write.

Where to begin, I guess you probably don't want me to drag on about where we went, but I will tell you that Crater Lake, Tahoe, Sacramento, Big Sur, Monterey, Carmel, and San Francisco were sweet–and I have t-shirts from all of these places plus from the many stops in between. I've added several things to the list of things I will do with my life, including returning here when I'm older. Either with my future kids to show them the beauty of this life, or by myself to simply sit and enjoy a beautiful moment in time. Hopefully both.

I didn't know what to expect during the half marathon. I was back in the eleventh starting box, which is pretty far back, but there were 34 total starting boxes so at least I was placed in the top third of the field. The entire first mile of the race was just a mess. My eyes were racing from side to side trying to find open space so as not to trip myself or anyone else. I tried to tell myself to slow down, especially since it seemed that I was passing everybody and not being passed, but at the mile mark I was right on pace for where I wanted to be. Once the field thinned out and running space was no longer at a premium, I found myself focusing as I normally do when I run–stride, pace, breathing, etc.–only the scenery of Fisherman's Wharf captured my eye and my mind began to drift.

Drift to life back home. I'd be returning to it tomorrow, and two weeks had flown by so quickly. Part of my mind concentrated on my changing relationships with my family. I genuinely felt bad about ditching my father over the summer and knew that I could make more of an effort. And Mom needed to see more of me, even if it meant that I simply sat home and watched a movie with her. Mark and I had enjoyed a peaceful summer absent from our normal blowouts and fisticuffs, but that was largely to the fact that we were rarely home at the same time. I'd enjoyed our trip to New York and decided that I would forge the olive branch and establish a more frequent line of communication. I know I needed to do that with Layne as well. Here I was his older brother, and the fact that we got along wasn't good enough. While running, I pledged to myself that I would be his older brother and become involved, especially since he was lacking the same thing I was lacking: a positive male role model on a daily basis.

And that took my mind into a new direction: Did I lack a positive male role model? No, I had Bennett and Blackwell. As a sophomore in high school, I had cried in Blackwell's room and practically begged him to be my father, but he always kept a bit of a distance, or so I thought. Blackwell gave me books to read to teach me the lessons that a boy needs to learn. He forced me to succeed and guided me, even when I didn't want to be guided. And the same could be said for Bennett. The man who I had cursed so violently just a few months ago was showing me the world. He called me on my weaknesses and wouldn't accept the same old bullshit that everyone else had allowed me to get away with.

I thought deeply about the lesson in *Last Wave*. Traditionally, Blackwell and I conversed on the books and he guided me through our conversations, seeing to it that I found the moral. But not this time, I knew I found it on my own: Life is short, live it, but live it well doing what is right and forging meaningful friendships, not surface relationships for personal gain. When my sophomore year began, I had surface relationships with people who I partied with. But I parted with them, and they didn't care; instead, for a while they tormented me until they grew tired of me ignoring it. But in the meantime, I had gained two friends, Forrest and Jennifer, that meant more to me than the rest of the previous group combined.

As I crossed the Golden Gate Bridge, my mind was interrupted by the dense fog and stiff breeze; I simply enjoyed the ride and recrossed it on the reverse loop with the same passion, this time enjoying the scent as well. On my initial crossing, Bennett passed me in the reverse direction, I figured he was about a mile ahead of me, but given that he started in box two, I wondered what our actual time differential was. For several minutes, I tried to figure out a reason why Bennett had opted out of the full marathon to run in the half, but in the end, I guess it doesn't really matter.

By the time I entered the neighborhoods of San Francisco on the last leg of the thirteen plus mile journey, I allowed my thoughts to drift to Jennifer. Perhaps it was exhaustion or an eerie sense of peace I felt through my solitude and the beauty around me, but I decided that I wouldn't worry about our relationship anymore. If she chose to be with me, then that was awesome, but if not, so be it. And I know it sounds like our earlier lunchroom contract, but this time I meant it. I know what I want to do with my life, and if she wants to join me, then I hope she will, but I cannot force her or will her to. Just like I won't let someone will their future upon me. In my heart, I hope Jennifer will sit right beside me from a cliff overlooking the Pacific or a hilltop looking down on Crater Lake, but if she doesn't join me, then at the very least I will always have a friend to tell about my experiences to. And I decided that I didn't need to tell Jennifer about this new ideology. Rather, I would see where time took us and where she wanted to go, because who knows, maybe her future was intertwined with mine, but I just don't know it yet.

And that thought fixed in my mind for a while, until the roar of the crowd indicated I was nearing the finish line. A broad smile engulfed my face as I tore for the chute, I knew the race clock was partially inaccurate since I started in box eleven, and as I looked at my watch I clocked myself at an hour and twenty three minutes plus six seconds (officially, I lost a second). I quickly found Bennett waiting for me; I think he was shocked to see me so soon. Both of us had figured he'd destroy me, but he didn't, in fact he beat me by just a little over a minute. Upon this knowledge, Bennett simply told me I'm going to be a star someday.

I looked to the bright morning sky, imagined darkness, and tried to pick where in the sky I wanted to lodge.

July 29, 2002

I can't sleep tonight, I'm thinking jet lag is the culprit, but it may be something else, I'll explain it in a second. It's just about midnight, but I'm not even close to tired. I want to play guitar, but that would wake the whole house and Mom and Mark need to rise early for work tomorrow.

Flying home today gave me mixed emotions. Part of me was sad to come home, not because home was bad, but because this trip had been so awesome. Everyday a new journey with new experiences. I yearn for that in my daily life. I know that few people enjoy such a life, most of us follow a daily routine and only break it on a rare occasion. But I will find my own path in life. I know I can't do it now with school and running, but just maybe after I graduate I can find my path, my own unique journey.

Behind the security lines at the airport, Mom was waiting all alone, peering through the crowd trying to find me. In her hands she held a newspaper, I couldn't fathom why she brought a newspaper to the airport, but I quickly found out.

While waiting for our luggage, Mom told me that Bennett had called the local newspaper and alerted them of our trip. In her hand was a small write up about the San Francisco race as well as Bennett's and my participation in it. Mom indicated that the newspaper called to set up a time to run a feature story on me. I promised Mom that I would try to act normal.

Pulling into the driveway, I hopped out to welcome home high-fives from my brothers and Forrest, plus a well deserved hug from Jennifer. Forrest had to go to work and Jennifer was baby sitting, so they could only stay for a few minutes, plus Mom told me on the drive home that she was taking us out for lunch. Just the three of us–Bennett, Mom, me.

And lunch is where that something else comes into play. I mean I should have seen it coming, but I put on blinders with the best of them when I truly want to.

"I think it's time for you to know that Coach Bennett and I are going to be spending some more time together," Mom began.

"What do you mean?" I replied with multiple gears turning inside my head at warp speed.

"Well," Mom continued, "over the last couple of months we've gone out for lunch several times and spent a few evenings together. We wanted to tell you because we know that he's your coach and things may get said that you don't want to hear."

My head was spinning. My mother and my coach–might I point out a twelve year age difference too with Mom on the older side of the swing–dating. Don't get me wrong, I want my mother to be happy, but this was bothering me. I couldn't help but think of how quickly my relationship had turned with Bennett: from shunned underachiever to golden child in a span of just a few weeks.

So I had to ask him, "Did you use me to get to my mother?"

Bennett nearly choked, "What do you mean Andrew?"

"A few months ago you hated me, now you're taking me across country giving me the start treatment."

"After I called your Mom about your grades a few months back, we stayed in touch," Bennett calmly began. "One day, we met for lunch to discuss why your grades were so important. I told her that you are the best runner I've ever seen, but you needed the grades not only to run here, but beyond high school too."

"And," Mom cut in, "it turns out that we had a lot in common; so we started meeting for lunch every week. We didn't tell you, Andrew, because we didn't want things to be strange for you; especially after Harris died."

Their explanation continued back and forth like this for a while. I absorbed a lot. And many loose ends tied themselves up neatly. Of course Mom wasn't surprised Bennett had asked me to travel the country with him–she knew about it before I ever did and feigned surprise. Similarly, she had convinced Bennett to take the train one way knowing full well that it would be a way to attract me to the idea. Clearly, this is how Mom played Dad off so well. She was going to let me spend time with Bennett regardless of Dad's opinion. What came most clear, however, was the fact that Mom thought this would be a great way for Bennett and me to see who we truly were as people. And that worked. Throughout the trip, all of the barriers between coach and student broke down–they had to. What formed in their place was a friendship. And if he was to be more involved in my life, and my mother's, than that relationship needed to be established. True, he needed that with my brothers too, but Mark was away at school most of the year and Layne attended a different school. Bennett was my coach and saw me daily in a completely different setting; he needed to establish a new setting, and Mom knew that too.

Eventually, they stopped talking and both of them stared at me expecting some sort of reply. Scores of thoughts and ideas paraded through my mind, but the dominant thought centered around Mom. If she was happy, I could be too and accept their relationship without animosity.

"Alright," I gathered myself, "do me a favor coach, at practice just treat me like everybody else."

"I plan on it, Andrew," was his response.

Lying in bed, I want to pretend that I'm cool with this, but I'm not sure that I am. My head spins like a planet around the sun, but there's nothing I can do about it. Plus, if Mom is happy, I should be happy for her, especially given all that she's sacrificed. But of all the men in the world, why did she have to choose my cross country coach?

I called Jennifer while she was babysitting and swore her to secrecy about the relationship. I had to tell somebody. Jennifer playfully laughed, but also agreed that Mom deserved to be happy.

After hanging up with Jennifer, I selfishly wished for their success, because maybe Bennett was also the man that I needed most in my life. After all, he was the man who demanded my best in the classroom, on the track, and in life. Nobody demanded the best of me in every aspect of my life.

Except Bennett.

August 4, 2002

Family dinner was a little different tonight; Bennett was there. I could tell he was nervous. Obviously he knew me, but Layne and Mark were a different story. Layne, of course, gave the whole indifferent routine while Mark put on heirs and tried to engage in meaningful conversation about business and that gig.

Mom too was visibly distracted. She dressed more elegantly and smiled more often. It was clear that this was a trial, but at just exactly what I'm still not sure of. Too soon for them to be thinking about this being how family dinners would be–right? But maybe this was Mom's way of testing all of our reactions or seeing if Bennett was truly up to the challenge of dating a woman with three kids. But in the end, things went well and jokes and casual conversation took over once the meal was blessed and the food scattered among the plates.

August 7, 2002

Instead of hitting the beach with Forrest today, I sat down with Heather Raines of the local newspaper. I'm not going to lie to you, I was nervous as all hell. I didn't want to say something that would make me look stupid, but at the same time I wanted to be myself.

Before the interview began, Heather produced two tape recorders. She said one tape was for her so she could write the story and that the other was for me so I could remember what I said and not feel misquoted when the article came out. Heather asked me many questions about how I train, ranging from diet to workout to weight training and sleep schedules. These questions were very easy as I was able to tell her about my daily runs, impeccable diet, and guaranteed eight hours of sleep a night.

But it was when she got to what makes me tick that truly unnerved me. I knew at some point I'd have to deal with this type of question; I'd seen it in the papers before, yet I still was entirely unprepared to answer it. At first, I wanted to answer the question philosophically, but come on, I'm just some kid and I'd look idiotic in the paper. So then I went for the straight truth, and the truth is that I barely know what makes me tick.

So here's the response, I gave, "Ummm, well I guess, what makes me tick is kind of you know what makes everyone tick. Kind of how some people love collecting stamps, I love running. Ummm, huh, well because when I'm running, you know, I kind of have that opportunity to clear my head and think about whatever it is that I want to think about, you know. And when I'm done running I feel better physically, mentally, and emotionally because I've cleared my head of everything that I've been thinking about." Pure eloquence, hopefully Heather will clean up my stumbling.

Here's where I blew it though, Heather followed up with, "So, Andrew, what do you think about when you're running?"

And I'm not sure if I panicked or just finally became myself. "Life," my response began, "I think about life. Some days I think about what type of girl I want my girlfriend to be, you know, really simple. Other days I try to solve life's mysteries, like how human life began on Earth and just why does water freeze from the top down while most other substance freeze from the bottom up. But most days, Heather, I just think about where I'm going. I think about all of the things I want to do in life and how little time I have to accomplish them. I set goals for myself and then when I'm done running I set a plan to make them happen. Like this summer I came up with a list of places I wanted to visit, so I set a schedule of when to visit them and I held myself to it, even if nobody else would go with me. I think about life when I run."

I can't wait to see the article, because I'm either going to love it or hate it, and I'm anxious to see how Heather perceived our conversation for I will be represented by her words, not my own, which is the irony of a story about myself. The article comes out on Thursday, August 15th as part of the paper's cross country preview.

August 10, 2002

It's been a week and time has passed pretty much the same as before I left for the west coast. Daily games of beach volleyball, working at the grocery store, and hanging out with Forrest, Jennifer, and Lisa.

Summer is coming to a close and I've accomplished much of what I set out to do, including Block Island, New York, and New London, but there is still so much more that I want to accomplish, not just this summer, but in life.

I had this wild thought today–which was Dad's day–so while I was driving back to Mom's house, I thought about cross country practice starting on Monday, and how I didn't want to go. I know this seems absurd given the recent race in San Francisco combined with the amount of time I've put into training. But it's not cross country that I resent, rather, it's the idea of going back to school. I guess it's typical for teenagers to claim they hate going to school, but that's not it. In fact, I don't mind school at all, and for the most part I enjoy my classes; I love English and social studies plus I'm fascinated by science, even though I'm not really good at it. Math, though, is a different story, I perform terribly in math class; it's not that I hate being there, it's just that I don't ever do well in math. Anyway, I'm just not ready to go back to school. I'd rather spend a few more months, perhaps a year, accomplishing other things. I want to walk into the woods and meditate for days while living off of the land. I want to sit on the sand of the Pacific and Atlantic and play guitar while writing, perhaps poetry. I want to travel to every state and explore the history of each one of them, both the good and the bad. I yearn to see how the Native Americans lived and how they've been robbed of their heritage. I want to experience so much, but I cannot do that inside of the four walls of a classroom.

Mom tells me to be patient, and all things I want will come in time so long as I never lose sight of my dreams and desires.

I know she's right. I need my education and I need my priorities. But patience is still something that I'm learning.

Some days I see myself spiritually connecting with the earth. We become one and are united. And through this unification we grow together, and touch others while sharing all that is good and celebrating life and what Earth has to offer.

I want that day now. But it must wait. Some days, I worry that I'll never reach that point in my life. Like today.

August 12, 2002

Practice started at dawn this morning, well 6:59 to be exact. Bennett likes using strange numbers so that everyone remembers where to be and when.

I walked onto the track not knowing what to expect. Here was Bennett collecting my paperwork like I was nobody special, which I appreciated. But at the same time I knew it was a charade. After all, this is the same man who is now dating my mother and took me across country to see the west coast and run in a race. How could I be just another runner?

Bennett solved that dilemma by introducing me to the team as the captain. Usually, we have a couple of captains, but Bennett made it clear that he was waiting to see who else would emerge as a leader. Truly, I'm not sure what I'd done to become captain. Being a top runner shouldn't be enough to warrant captaincy, but as Bennett explained to the team, I demonstrated positive attitude, effort, and commitment.

As I lead the team through stretching, I wondered incessantly about how my teammates viewed me. I'd learned not to care what others thought of me, but I wanted to be respected as a captain and not laughed at. I wanted my teammates to believe in me and trust in me. I didn't want them to see me as Bennett's lackey. Having Jennifer at practice certainly helped as she rallied the girls to cheer for me once the announcement was made.

The beauty of high school athletics is that every year a new group of athletes join the fray completely oblivious to what they're getting themselves into. Freshmen. And as soon as drills and warm-ups were over, a half dozen freshmen had crowded around me asking questions about running, stretching, and shoes. They knew no better. It felt good having the answers. A couple of the older guys slapped me five and congratulated me. They talked of district championships and the state meet. I simply told them that we were going to make that happen. As I glanced at my teammates, none of whom were my friends–save Jennifer, I felt a kindred bond unlike no other. We had a common goal and needed each other to make it happen. And that is the beauty of sport.

August 15, 2002

Bennett started practice by reading to the team the article that appeared in today's newspaper previewing the upcoming cross country season. I had already read it at home while eating a light breakfast. The article focused largely on our boys' team calling us the odds on district favorite with an outside chance of placing in the top three at the state meet. Our girls' team was largely ignored, though they too should compete for the district crown.

Bennett told us how such a write up sets the bar high and creates both opportunity and tension. He instructed us to ignore both the positive and negative press as both could affect us mentally. Instead, he wanted us to focus on the task at hand, whether it be practice, school, or a meet. It sounds simple, but it's much easier said than done when the very next breath he utters includes turning the page to read the pull down article about me. Scared and self conscious, I avoided reading the article while eating breakfast. So as Bennett read the article aloud, I too was hearing it for the first time, much like the vast majority of teammates, if not all of them.

I must hand it to Heather, she had a vision of how she wanted to portray me and she held onto that vision throughout the article, perhaps even lying at times. Repeatedly, she referred to me as composed and grounded. I'm not necessarily sure how she garnered those conclusions given our meeting, but the words that appeared on the page reinforced her declarations. Gone were all of the awkward pauses, mumblings, and stammers. All that remained were a few short phrases worked into Heather's meticulously written preambles. Suddenly I said that "I love running [because] it gives me the opportunity to clear my head." and how I use running "to set goals for myself."

At the conclusion of the article, Bennett insisted on praising me for how I took the lessons of cross country and applied them to life. "Notice how Andrew uses running to set goals for himself in life. Just like you guys have personal and team goals on the course, you should be doing the same at home and at school."

I felt awkward and unnecessarily singled out: I was worried how my teammates would respond once Bennett released me. Thankfully, most of them just went about business as usual, but the few who approached me said they felt the same things I spoke of in the article. And with that, I knew I wasn't alone. I'd just been too reticent to share it with anyone, except Jennifer.

Driving Jennifer home after practice, I told her how cool it was that I wasn't the only one who ran to clear my head and ponder life. She stared at me awkwardly almost as though she knew a deep, meaningful conversation was soon to follow.

Unfortunately for her, she was right. I opened up immediately and laid everything on the line. I told her about how much I missed her while I was traveling with Bennett and how her failure to promise to be by my side while we were stargazing in my backyard nearly destroyed me. I philosophized about the kinetic bond between two people and how in time she would see how much we were alike.

And that's when she cut me off and pointed out that I was only sixteen with an entire life in front of me and how unfair it was for me to put that type of pressure on her. I have to admit, I was ranting on and not even sure of what I was saying, but I wanted to convince her to love me and be with me forever, even if I was only sixteen and she fifteen.

Finally, I asked her point blank, "What do you think of me and what kind of relationship do you think we should have?"

"I knew this is where you were going, Andrew," Jennifer began, "and I've been asking myself that question for months, especially while you were gone this summer."

"What did you come up with for an answer?"

"I decided that if you ask me out on a date that I'll happily say yes. And that when you kiss me that I'll excitedly kiss you back. Do you remember when we used to hug and kiss each other? I miss that, and while I missed your closeness, I grew closer to you in other ways and have come to admire your uniqueness and love it."

Without hesitating, I asked Jennifer is she would go out with me on Saturday. And while she was in the process of saying yes, I pulled the car into the shoulder, took off my seatbelt, leaned across the seat, and kissed her gently on her lips.

Jennifer kissed me back, just as she said she would, only with a tear in her eye that I did not expect.

August 17, 2002

Mark left for school this morning. Unlike times past when I welcomed his departure, I felt a tug of sorrow at his leaving. We had a good summer together, though we barely saw each other, which probably contributed to our friendliness.

As Dad's car pulled away, I sat on the steps thinking about our relationship. At first, I focused solely on the bad days, like Mark shaking his head in disgust when I had a bad race or him yelling at me for not understanding his diatribes regarding our family. But those memories took on a new clarity. Instead, as Mark and Dad filtered into the distance, I thought about how Mark perceived himself. He is the oldest brother and the oldest male in a female lead household. Perhaps he felt like somebody needed to take charge, maybe that's why he orders for us when out in public. And that further explains the pressure that Mark always put on me to be successful, after all, isn't that the job of the man of the house? To demand the best of everyone and be tough about it? But Mark didn't know how to also be gentle about it, as a true man should be. But how can I hold that against him? He had nobody to learn from and his only memories of how it should be done ring with strident arguments and broken promises.

He did the best he could.

At some point this summer Mark came to respect my oddity. He appreciated my dedication to running and my commitment to the life I want to live. Mark, too, is committed to the life he believes in and doesn't allow people to stand in his way. I learned to respect that. Though our dreams travel opposite paths orbiting in different directions, both of our dreams are powerful and desperate; neither one of us would ever allow them to be derailed. Mark knows that I will fail. And he's learned to accept that, just as I know that he will fail, something that I've known for quite a while. But it is in our greatest failures that we also find our greatest successes. I lost all of my friends, yet found myself. I lost the race, but found my stride. Mark lost his father, but found his future. We talked about that, how we could learn from mistakes and not hold grudges. Mark didn't fully agree with me, but at least he's trying. It made me feel good that he proactively talked to Mom and Dad about Thanksgiving in November. He set a schedule, sound familiar, and he's comfortable with that. So am I.

When I picked Jennifer up tonight, I had no plan. True, I was starving, but I'm always hungry so stopping to eat is just a given. Luckily Jennifer had refrained from eating figuring I'd want to eat.

We grabbed a table at a downtown café and sat on the sidewalk, watching scores of people from many different outlooks pass us by. Families, grandparents, newlyweds, college kids, and our classmates skate boarded, walked, ran, and drove by. I love to people watch, as does Jennifer, and we talked extensively about those we knew and created stories about the strangers.

As the server cleared dessert, we were both ready to leave and catch sunset at the beach. It was there we truly connected, just the two of us stretched out, backs against the sand, eyes set on the horizon. And that's where we went, to the horizon. Though I'm sure some watched us awkwardly from afar, to me, we were alone on the beach, reconnecting, holding and kissing each other just like we've always been meant to do.

I'd almost forgotten how gentle Jennifer's body was and how sweet her breath tasted, but it rushed back to my senses, carrying my spirits away. It was pitch dark when we left, hand in hand, no plan in sight.

We grabbed a movie and crashed at her parents' house, right on the sofa, where Jennifer's mom played out the continual charade of ducking in every ten minutes with food, drinks, or random questions. I had forgotten about this part of our relationship.

But her mom tired and left us to slip underneath an old family quilt holding each other tightly watching a movie that neither of us cared about.

And as I awoke in the middle of the night, I didn't want to move. I knew I wasn't home, but I didn't know if I was alone. I carefully moved my fingers, turned my head, and gently kissed Jennifer as she slept next to me on her parents' couch. I knew I'd have some explaining to do in the morning, but I didn't care. And for once, I didn't have to pretend to be happy.

New Beginnings

August 21, 2002

I locked the car, wandered towards the school's entrance, and checked to make sure that I had everything I needed for the day, especially my lunch given our cafeteria's notorious past.

I walked slowly, mostly thinking about how this school year would go, my junior year. According to my teachers, parents, and guidance counselors, this was to be my most important year academically, as far as college was concerned at least.

But I see this year as being important for other reasons. Instead of opening a door that only leads to a repetitious cycle of classes, work, and practice, I decided to open a door that leads to opportunity. My girlfriend was a year younger than me and would share no common classes or lunches. My best friend, Forrest, attended a private school. None of this bothered me. Being me was alright. The more I opened myself up to my true self, the more I found myself interacting with others. Finally, my brother Mark and I had a descent relationship. Teammates sought my advice and even invited me to hangout at their pool or grab a movie with them after practice. I once thought that I had lost myself in order to find myself. But in reality, I was never truly lost and I will never truly find myself. Both are eternally evolving and there's no such thing as being lost, all 'missed' turns are part of the path, whether we know it or not.

And as I opened the door to start a new school year, I also opened a door that was the clearest vision of me.

www.ingramcontent.com/pod-product-compliance
Lightning Source LLC
La Vergne TN
LVHW090939080826
845145LV00003B/813

* 9 7 8 0 5 7 8 0 0 6 3 6 9 *